FIRE SONG

ADAM GARNET JONES

D0621087

annick press
toronto + berkeley

Fire Song by Adam Garnet Jones is based on the film *Fire Song*
produced by Fire Song Films Inc. and Big Soul Productions Inc.
and written and directed by Adam Garnet Jones

Designed by Emma Dolan
Cover images courtesy of istock.com:
Night Sky © Jamesteohart; Friends © Antolikjan

Fire Song takes place in Canada and as such Shane refers to the land he lives on
as the `reserve'; in the U.S., the more common term is `reservation.' Commonly used
Anishinaabemowin words and phrases that appear throughout the story are set in italics.

We acknowledge the support of the Canada Council for the Arts and the
Ontario Arts Council, and the participation of the Government of Canada/la
participation du gouvernement du Canada for our publishing activities.

Cataloging in Publication

Jones, Adam Garnet, author
　　　Fire song / Adam Garnet Jones.
Issued in print and electronic formats.
ISBN 978-1-55451-978-1 (hardcover).–ISBN 978-1-55451-977-4 (softcover).–
ISBN 978-1-55451-980-4 (PDF).–ISBN 978-1-55451-979-8 (EPUB)
　　　I. Title.
PS8619.O524F57 2018　　　　jC813'.6　　　　C2017-905509-7
　　　　　　　　　　　　　　　　　　　　　　　　　C2017-905510-0

Published in the U.S.A. by Annick Press (U.S.) Ltd.
Distributed in Canada by University of Toronto Press.
Distributed in the U.S.A. by Publishers Group West.

www.annickpress.com
www.adamgarnetjones.com

Also available as an e-book. Please visit www.annickpress.com/ebooks.html
for more details.

For the ones we lost, and for the ones who fight to stay

CHAPTER ONE

Shane is awake, wishing he wasn't. The alarm clock makes a soft warning click before flooding the room with staticky Top 40. *Too loud.* Shane reaches an arm out from under the covers and hits snooze for the third time. It feels better in bed. Not good, but better. As long as his door is closed, no one wants anything from him. No one is asking if he's okay, *as if he'd tell them the truth anyways.* He'll have to make a move eventually, but if he can coax himself into a Drift, he can delay a little longer.

Sometimes when he's upset, the Drift comes in and takes him out like a rogue wave. *Whooooosh*—he's somewhere else. Other days, if he can get his mind to stop spinning and if he breathes in the right way, he can call the Drift in. Shane takes a long sip of air, praying for it to fill every unseen part of him. When his chest starts to burn, he lets out the breath in a gentle, focused stream. The Drift begins as a tingle. It starts in his fingertips, then creeps up his arms and over the tender flesh of his neck until it blooms over his eyelids and bursts into a constellation of squirming silver pinpricks that fill his field of vision. Warmth pulses through his center and guides him out of his body. If only his whole life could have the rush of sweetness that comes during a Drift, when the weight of his limbs drops away and the purest part of him rises high up through the dripping ceiling and out over the top of his house.

He floats above the tree line and passes into that magic half-way-place between the earth and the sky. Even on his worst days, the snaking line of the creek and the tree-furred shores of the silver water can stop his heart. It's the home of his ancestors. The place of prophecy, where food grows upon the water. A place where, if you can fly away from the level of the earth and see it all with the eyes of a crow, there will always be balance. No matter how much struggle is skewing the edges of the circle down below. Maybe that's what his sister was looking for—the eyes of a crow at the end of a rope. *Stop thinking of her,* Shane tells himself. He shifts his attention to the breeze blowing over his face and lets it rinse the thought clean away.

Shane floats out over the houses; first the little old ones like his that have been here the longest, and then on to the crisp siding and double-glazed windows of the bigger places built by people with money. The edge of the reserve is dotted with trailers. People on TV talk about trailers like they are the crap, but Tara's is bigger than Shane's house. And if you want to you can pick them up and move them anywhere you want. Not that he's ever seen one move once it got put down. People are that way too, unless you have your eyes on school. Most people think that if you're smart, you won't stick around long. And if you graduate and don't take off to the city then you probably don't have much to offer the band anyway. One time Roberta, the school counselor, told Shane that education is like the golden ticket Charlie found in *Charlie and the Chocolate Factory*. Shane mentioned it to Tara later and she said that a kid who licks wallpaper and ends up living with a crazy old man in a purple velvet suit isn't such a great role model. She may be right.

The wind changes and Shane Drifts over the dirt road that leads to the sun-bleached wooden benches of the powwow grounds, where the air meets the water at the edge of the lake. People from all over gather here at the height of summer to catch up with faraway family, to show off new babies and new regalia, to sing and dance and laugh and eat, and snag. But even when there's no one there, the powwow grounds have the shine of the people lighting it up from the inside. It's like the room of a dying man or the ground where a midwife stands, reaching into the edge of the spirit world. Sacred, you know? His sister, Destiny, was almost crowned powwow princess here last year. She would have been, too, if she had taken the time to braid her hair and finish the details on her regalia the way the other girls did. The judges probably thought she didn't care enough. But she did care. Not about pulling her hair back or finishing the hemline of her regalia. She just wanted to dance. And she had more grace, more of the healing power of that jingle dress dance, in her than anyone he's ever seen. Shane loved watching her feet move like a whisper over the ground, impossibly soft and quick, almost floating in her moccasins. She was so …

And just like that he's back in his bed again, eyes bulging, and gasping for air like a pickerel flipped onshore. There's nothing like the half-awake peace of forgetting for a few minutes that your little sister is dead, before reality busts in and pisses all over everything. Shane had felt sad and angry when people in his family and community passed on to the spirit world, but nothing could have prepared him for the sick heat that has been twisting in his guts since the night Destiny did it. No one tells you how much you can hurt and still look normal on the outside.

Shane takes deep breath after deep breath, trying to get into another Drift, but it's no use. He's not going anywhere. A drop of gray water hangs from the ceiling. It gathers moisture from the soggy drywall, growing and drooping until it splashes into an overflowing bucket. Ripples race out to touch the edges of the bucket, and then disappear. Shane watches the drops grow heavy and fall, each transforming into the energy of tiny waves that dissipate into nothingness. David would see those ripples and say that everything is alive. Shane's science teacher would say that energy never dies. The idea is the same, but nothing explains what happens when those ripples crash against the wall and the water goes flat.

The hot steam of the shower lets Shane pretend for a few more minutes that the world is a bad dream. When he steps out, water runs down the tips of his shaggy hair and falls on his wide brown shoulders. He accidentally catches his own eyes in the mirror and quickly turns away. Looking in your own eyes can mess you up when you're lying to yourself that everything is going to be okay.

Shane pulls out his mourning outfit for the memorial. Black sneakers with black pants and the black button-up shirt that only gets worn when someone dies. The fabric pulls tight over his chest, gaping a little around the top button when he stands with his shoulders straight. It will have to do. After Destiny died, going to the city for a new shirt was the last thing on his mind.

Things like a shirt being a little small—the normally insignificant details of life that go unnoticed by everyone else—have a habit of crawling under his skin and latching on. He never feels right unless everything is where and how it's supposed to be. But now that Destiny is gone, something will always be wrong. He will feel the stab of her absence in every passing moment, forever.

Shane notices a gray smudge on his elbow. He turns to search for something to wipe it with. His mother would say, *Quit fussing like that. Boys should be a little bit messy.* As far as Shane can tell, being a boy—or being the right kind of boy—has something to do with not caring. It has to do with leaping without looking and speaking without choosing your words. And so after one too many comments like *Why are you standing with your hands on your hips?* Shane tried to leave the dishes undone every once in a while. He tried to abandon stray hairs in the sink, to aim a few splashes of urine over the lip of the toilet. But it didn't come naturally, and he could never figure out how much was too much.

Then one day a white lady on TV said, *When getting dressed for the day, every woman should remove one unnecessary item from her outfit.* That gave him an idea. He stopped trying to leave spontaneous messes, and returned to cleaning his room and dressing as usual, but with one small change. Before leaving his room each day, Shane would throw a shirt or a stack of books on the floor. He did the same thing with his clothes. He made sure everything was clean and matching, then threw it off by wearing one sock in an odd color, or messing his hair up a bit, just in case his mom got to feeling like he wasn't messy enough to be a real boy. Since Destiny died he hasn't had to try. The mess has multiplied as though a door were left open and their home has been taken over by careless, slovenly ghosts. Dirty laundry festers in small damp piles. Dishes lie molding in the sink.

And suddenly she's there. Destiny. Sitting on the edge of the bed in ripped goth-girl fishnets. Their eyes meet, and it's like hangover soup in winter. Her warmth fills him up and drapes itself around his heart. Shane takes in a shaky breath. It hurts to miss her this much. Destiny laughs and tells him he looks like an undertaker. "Why so serious!?" she says in her best Joker voice. He smiles. She always knew how to make him feel better. He holds her eyes with his, counting down the seconds until his breathing returns to normal and he's left alone in the room again. It's the same way each time—she comes in a moment of panic and then washes away like a dream. Shane once heard an old man on the radio talking about how his arm got ripped off in a farming accident. But even after the man knew his arm was gone, even half a lifetime later, he could still feel it attached to his body. When Shane heard that, he thought the old guy was just making a play for attention. Now he knows. Just because something is gone doesn't mean it isn't there. Shane's brain understands that he'll never joke with his sister again, but his blood and bones and spirit refuse to accept it. Goddamn it hurts.

The blast of a horn from the driveway startles him. It's Uncle Pete come to drive him and his mom to the school for the memorial.

Shane stops outside the door to his sister's room. It's covered in stickers and drawings and a sign with *Destiny* written in bubble letters. "Mom?" No answer. Shane pushes the door open gently. Soft light streams in through a gap in the purple curtains. Destiny liked it to be dark in there. In better days their mom, Jackie, always burst into Destiny's room and tugged the curtains open, insisting that sunlight is the fifth food group. Destiny would flop onto her bed, shrieking and flailing her arms like a vampire being exposed to sunlight. And she would keep it up—her record was ten straight minutes of dramatic hissing and clawing at the air—until Jackie closed them again. *That's my little bloodsucker,* Jackie would say, kissing the top of Destiny's head.

Jackie is there in the room now, slumped over like part of the bedding. Since Destiny died, his mother's face and hair have fallen slack, like a flag without wind. Evie sits quietly next to her. She's watching Jackie from behind thick glasses that make her eyes appear much smaller, giving her the face of a wise old mole. Evie probably seems like she's Shane's grandmother but she's not—his grandmothers are long gone—but anybody who's got trouble in their life and who doesn't let the church boss them around goes to Evie for help. That's what elders do.

Shane puts his hand on Jackie's shoulder. She presses her face into his hip and begins to cry, saying something that sounds like *I'msorryI'msorryI'msorryI'msorryI'msorry,* but it might not even be words at all. Evie reaches out and rubs Jackie's back.

"I know, Mom. It's okay." Shane picks up her stiff black flats. "Here. Let's get these on you." Jackie pulls away and curls her feet under the bed like a child. Shane watches the jumbled shapes and lines of her face, searching for clues that will help him predict what's coming. It's like learning how to read all over again, but dangerous.

"No—I'm not going. I don't need everybody looking at me like that."

"Like what?"

"You know ..."

"They just want to help. They just want you to feel better." Jackie frowns, running her fingernails over her scalp. "C'mon, Mom. We need to go. It'll only be an hour." Shane takes her elbow to help her up. Jackie twists away from him and tumbles back on the bed.

"I'm not going! What's wrong with you!?" Jackie looks at Shane's neat black clothes as if seeing him for the first time. "Who're you trying to impress, anyways?"

The house shakes with the weight of Uncle Pete's footsteps on the kitchen floor. *Not now,* Shane thinks. He's had enough trouble getting his mom moving without Pete in the way. If only Shane could put him into a press, shrink him down until he's too small to do any damage. The size of a car battery or a bag of road salt. If Shane were in Pete's place, he would feel his sister's loss and imagine her ragged nerves. He would attempt some small measure of grace, considering. He would leave his boots at the door.

"C'mon, Jacks, it's time to go," Pete barks as he clomps his way through the kitchen, rattling the dishes in their shelves and filling up the door to Destiny's room like a swollen cork in a bottle.

Jackie's face twists up at him. "Get outta here, Pete! I don't want you in this room. No one should even be in this room."

Pete sucks in a big breath of air, ready to dig into Jackie the way he would any other day, but Evie stops him with a gentle touch of her hand on his shoulder. Pete would probably love to shove her hand away and give her a piece of his mind too, but he knows he can't. That's granny power. Pete shakes his head like a drunk fighting off sleep, then stomps out mumbling, "I'll be waiting."

Evie settles into a chair across from Jackie and clears her throat. "I brought something for you."

Jackie looks up. "I don't need anything." Evie pulls a small brown leather pouch from her bag and holds it out for Jackie. Shane has seen it before. Evie keeps it full of the sacred medicines—cedar, sage, sweetgrass, and tobacco.

"This'll protect you from that bad spirit." Jackie's eyes pass over the leather, dark and shiny from its time in ceremony.

"Take it, Mom."

For Shane's whole life, the first thing they did after having a pee and brushing their teeth in the morning was smudge with a mix of white sage and sweetgrass that they had picked with Evie and David in the summers. They would gather together in the front window while Jackie lit the smudge and bathed herself in the smoke. Shane loved seeing the white smoke curling up over the soft curve of their mother's shoulders; they loved the flutter of her eyelids as she prayed. When she was finished, Jackie would hold the smudge bowl for Shane and fan the embers with a feather. Destiny always prayed last; she liked to bury the ashes under one of the big trees in the yard. All that stopped when Destiny died. No more medicines. No more ceremony. Another thing lost. Evie extends her arm to Jackie. "Take it." Shane silently wills Jackie to reach out for the medicines, but Jackie pushes the bag away. The corners of Evie's mouth droop.

"Shane! Let's go!" Pete calls from outside the house.

Shane lingers at the threshold of his sister's room. "See you later, Mom." Jackie doesn't look up. "I won't be long."

Evie raises her hand and nods the way only grandmothers can, putting him at ease and letting him know his mom will be taken care of while he's gone. Shane scans the room, taking note of the humps of laundry at the foot of the bed, and the dirty dishes that he will have to pick up and wash after the memorial.

*

Scrubby trees and houses flash by the window of Uncle Pete's truck. Shane has seen it all a million times. Some days it feels like everything around him—Janice's store that sits like a fat blue bead on the main road, the familiar faces that nod hello as they pass by, the cracked siding of the band office, the bleached silver planks of the powwow grounds—all of it is part of his skin. The people, the buildings, the gravel, and the trees have all lived together for so long they are indistinguishable from one another. His heart beats under this ground and the roots of the trees spread through his lungs. He is his home. But today this place feels like a crappy video game with only one level, where he just keeps passing the same shrubs and beat-up houses over and over again in an endless, cheaply made loop. It's these dirt roads that wash out in spring, the mail that's always getting lost, the unreliable water system—all of it sparked his interest in urban planning and his drive to go to school. He loves going over new plans for parks, sewage systems, transit systems, anything designed to move people and organize their lives. It was inspiring to feel like the answers to the problems he's grown up with all seem to be out there, waiting for him.

Uncle Pete has been talking since they left his house. "How much longer you think she's gonna be like that?"

"I don't know. You're her brother—you tell me." Uncle Pete gives him some side-eye.

"Well, you seem to be doing okay. I don't know why she can't pull it together. My auntie lost one son to suicide, one daughter was murdered." Shane glares through the window, trying to block Pete out. "She never once holed up like that. She just kept working. But your mom, always thought the world owed her something. When things don't go her way, that's it."

"She just needs time," says Shane, still looking out the window.

"Pfffft. She needs a smack is what she needs."

Shane digs his nails into his palms and pushes his fist into the upholstery, forcing himself not to rise to his uncle's bait. Pete chews on the ends of his wispy mustache and turns up the radio. The truck slows as they approach a stop sign. Shane quickly calculates the likelihood of Uncle Pete saying something to push him over the edge in the five minutes it's going to take to get from here to the school. He decides not to chance it.

The truck stops, and Shane jumps out. He slams the door, and takes long strides down the dirt road without looking back. Pete's truck follows at a crawl behind him.

Uncle Pete yells, "What—you gonna be pissed at me now?" The truck's tires roll over the gravel with a soft crunch, like someone trying to walk quietly in the bush. "Look at you with your nose in the air, all in a huff. I can tell you were raised without a man around."

Shane looks at Pete sharply. "You got that right."

For a moment it looks like Pete might stop the truck and give Shane a pounding, but he guns the engine and takes off. Shane steps onto the shoulder to avoid the spray of gravel.

CHAPTER TWO

When Shane arrives at the school, the parking lot is full. The whole rez is here. Usually there's no one around on the last day of the school year, but a memorial brings out a crowd. Cars line the roadside like a huddled row of boulders planted by giants. Everyone he knows is waiting inside to lift his family up. *Death brings us closer,* Shane thinks. It seems messed up, but today he's glad for it. He checks his phone to distract himself from the tears that keep itching at the corners of his eyes. The memorial was supposed to start half an hour ago. Thank god for Indian time— there's no way it's started yet.

Shane wipes at his eyes and approaches a group of girls who stand in a huddle smoking cigarettes and retouching their makeup. Tara is among them, quietly glowing, even with her ragged nail beds and stiff funeral clothes. She's got a notebook in her hands that she carries around with her everywhere. She never lets him look at it but she scribbles in it all the time. He asked her what she was doing once and she said she was writing hip-hop lyrics—she's gonna write a song and get rich. *Good luck with that one,* he'd said. Everybody's got a get-rich-quick scheme, seems like.

Ashley, a thick girl with a square face, frowns as she takes a deep drag from her smoke and nods at Shane. Tara breaks from the group and throws her arms around him.

"Are you okay?" she asks.

Shane nods. "Where's Kyle this morning?"

Ashley flicks her cigarette into the dirt. "His auntie won't let him come. She heard there was gonna be drumming and stuff. I don't know—she thinks if he hears it he'll go straight to hell or something."

Tara shakes her head. "That's just not right."

"And they say traditional people are the superstitious ones," Ashley smirks. They all laugh. It feels weird, but normal in a way. Destiny would have laughed too.

*

Only half of the fluorescent lights inside the gym are on. The place has a murky cave-like intimacy. A collapsible screen has been set up by the front and a slideshow of Destiny's life is being projected on it. Shane tries to watch but his guts get twisting again. The photos are from happy times. Snapshots. Moments frozen for the benefit of a future that, until recently, felt limitless. No one looks at the screen after snapping a selfie and says, *Yes, use that one at my funeral!* It feels morbid to have them here, as though after fifteen years of life, Destiny's suicide is the most meaningful thing that ever happened to her. *She's my sister—not a fucking cautionary tale,* Shane wants to say. Looking at pictures of her isn't going to somehow make it all make sense. And if anyone thinks it will, they're fooling themselves, as if rewriting their memories of Destiny so that her suicide seems inevitable will somehow protect them from tragedy. It won't. They can look all they want, but there's nothing to learn. Nowhere to hide. Shane stifles the urge to knock over the projector and grind the pieces to dust.

People stand around talking in quiet clusters, sipping weak tea from Styrofoam cups. Shane pulls his shoulders back and lifts his chin. They need to see that he isn't broken. That there is hope. They're here to show him support, but they need something from him too.

David catches his eye from across the room and gives him a small nod. He's tall and narrow and carries himself with his head slightly bent, like a long blade of grass with its tip curled over in the summer sun. Shane blinks and he's suddenly across the room, with his face pressed into the weedy warmth of David's neck. Everyone else disappears and it's like they're alone in his bedroom the way they used to be when Destiny was alive. When they kissed, it felt like they were a single spirit living in two skins. A blink later and Shane is back. Hushed voices echo off the high ceilings like a distant waterfall. He wishes David would push his way through the crowd of mourners and stand with him, but he knows him better than that. Maybe it's for the best. Shane can put up a front for Tara or Roberta or anyone else here, but David will see how close he is to breaking.

A group of Jackie's friends from work step cautiously toward Shane and Tara. One of them takes Shane's hand. "I'm so sorry, Shane."

"Thanks, Bev."

Joyce leans in. "How is your mom holding up? I dropped some food by your place but I didn't hear anything."

"She's not ready to see anyone yet."

Mary smiles at him in that way that lets you know the person is worried sick about you. It makes Shane feel like he should apologize, but he can't because then she would feel worse. "You're such a good son," Mary says.

"Thank you."

"You tell her we miss her down at the store."

"I will."

Tara tries to pull Shane to a seat near the front of the room. Roberta, the school counselor, waves Shane toward her. "Just a second," Shane says. "I'll be back." Tara looks around to see if anyone noticed that Shane left her alone.

As usual, Roberta is vibrating at a higher frequency than the rest of the room. Shane often wonders whether she would be happier if events like this were organized by someone else, or if she would actually be lost without something to obsess over. Roberta looks over Shane's shoulder. "Where's your mom?"

"She's not coming. Evie's with her." Shane notices David pretending to organize a plate of cookies just within earshot.

"Shit," Roberta says. "Evie was going to do the opening prayer. I'll have to see if I can get someone else."

"Just start, Roberta. It's fine."

"Maybe I can get Lucie White ..."

David steps forward. "I'll do it," he says.

Roberta sighs. "It's okay, David. I'm sure Lucie won't mind."

"It's okay. My *nookomis* taught me. I wanna do it, for Destiny."

Roberta hesitates.

"Thanks, David," Shane says. He squeezes David's shoulder, wishing they could have even five minutes, alone. David steps away before anything can pass between them.

*

Shane sits in the front row beside Tara. The plastic folding chair squeaks every time he shifts his weight, so he tries not to move at all. Tara reaches out and takes his hand between hers. He can feel her eyes on him. She's waiting for him to fall apart or show a hint of weakness. So far he's held her at bay, but once she finds a way in, she'll open that crack wider and wider. Eventually his whole body will bust open and she'll be knee-deep in blood and shit; she'll be so much a part of his messed-up life that he won't even be able to think about life without her. But at least she's there beside him. That counts for a lot. David would never hold his hand in public, no matter how much he needed it.

Roberta steps up to the podium. "Good morning, everyone. Thank you for coming. Elder Evie Thomas wanted to be here, but she was called away at the last minute this morning. Her grandson David will say the opening in her place." Roberta steps aside to make room for David at the podium. David looks up at the crowd. He glances at Roberta, then crosses his arms to his chest. Shane leans forward in his chair. *Come on, David.* After a moment, David wets his lips with his tongue and speaks into the microphone in a voice that is slow and steady.

"*Aanii. Boozhoo.* David Thomas *nindizhinikaaz. Chi miigwech* to all of you for being here, and to the school for choosing to remember Destiny on our last day here." David's voice wavers. "It's been six weeks since she, ah … took her life."

Shane's stomach lurches with the mention of his sister's name. He looks down at the picture of Destiny on the memorial program to block out David's voice. Her eyes tug at him like a winch pulling something dead out of the bush, winding his intestines into a tight coil. Shane tips forward in his chair and suddenly he's falling and floating at the same time. He's on a Drift. He rises up through the roof of the gym and away over the rez. The Drift picks up speed, dragging him farther than he's gone before—over a rippling ocean of trees and muskeg, over shale and granite waves until trees have been replaced by flat fields of rock and rugged, unbroken tundra.

He hurls a long scream into the bare silence of rock and ice. But the sound, so much smaller once it leaves his body, gets sucked up by the wind and disappears. His hungry lungs take gulps of air that burns cold and dry like peppermint. A sensation blows over his skin like wind. It creeps into him and taps a rhythm that grows until it's pounding inside his bones. It shudders through the land and surges in him with wild, inarticulate panic. Underneath the din an unfamiliar voice is whispering, *IneedtoliveIneedtoliveIneedtoliveIneedtolive* …

*

And then it's over. Shane sits alone in the empty gym, while Roberta and one of the teachers stack chairs against the wall, making the air shiver with the crash of metal and hard plastic. There must have been more to it—thank-yous from teachers and speeches about the inspiring futures of the tiny graduating class, but it's a blur. After all the pressure and the waiting and the anticipation—it's hard to believe this is it. He can just walk away from school and never come back. It should feel like an ending or a beginning but it doesn't feel like anything. It feels like another day without Destiny.

"Shane!"

Shane turns. Tara is standing in the doorway waiting.

"I thought you were going to meet me outside," she says. "Everyone's gone."

Shane gets up slowly, feeling a dull ache in all his muscles. He started going on Drifts when he was twelve or thirteen. It was just a few steps past daydreaming, and he could control it. But as he got older, they became more intense and less predicable. Now, they mostly take him without warning. And when he comes back, it feels like every muscle in his body has been clenched like a fist for a solid hour, leaving his limbs heavy with blood.

*

Shane and Tara stand at the end of a long point of land that reaches out into the lake. "You always smell so good." Tara nestles into him a little closer. Shane looks across the water. It isn't as windy as it usually is down here, but the grasses still whisper around them. He wishes Tara would leave him alone. He can feel her body listening to him, like every part of her is monitoring his responses and recording them for some unknown purpose. Fingertip surveillance.

"Is Evie still talking like some spirit killed Destiny?" Tara asks.

Shane bends down and picks up a handful of rocks. The cold and the grit of them feel too real to be part of the rest of his life right now. He chooses a round black stone, pulls his arm back, and throws it as hard as he can. It's a sloppy throw, but the rock curves out over the water like a ribbon unfurling before it taps the surface and drops away. Tara hooks a finger in his belt loop.

"I just feel like I should have seen something or known she was gonna do it."

Shane tenses. *Why does everyone feel like they get to comment on Destiny's death, like it's something from the news?* If she keeps this up he doesn't know how much longer he can be nice to her. No one has any idea why Destiny did it. She was sad. She was fucked up. They all knew it but they didn't know how deep it went. If he and David didn't see it, why would Tara?

"It's not your fault," Shane says. "Stop worrying about it." Another rock explodes from his fist, going higher and farther than the last one. Tara wraps his arm around her shoulder like an accessory. *Grief-stricken boyfriends are totally on-trend this season! They make other girls sorry for you and weirdly jealous at the same time!*

Tara pulls him close. "I tried to do it once. A couple years ago. I had a knife in my hand and I was ready to do it and everything."

Shane untangles himself from Tara. "That's not the same thing, is it?"

"I don't know."

"Well, you didn't do it, did you? So it's not the same thing."

Tara looks like she's lost something but can't remember what it is. "I just feel like I know what she was going through so I should have seen something, you know?

Shane frowns. "You never talked to her. You weren't even friends."

"Don't be mad."

"I'm not mad."

"Shane."

"I'm not mad. I'll text you later." He gives a wave without looking back, and walks up the path against the beginning of a wind. He knows he's being a shit, but it doesn't feel possible to turn back and apologize. It's not like their relationship has anywhere to go. Better to create distance one step at a time than to spring it on her all at once.

CHAPTER THREE

Feeling pretty down today. Shane being an asshole doesn't help, but I get it. Destiny's memorial was this morning. The whole thing went okay, but it's messed up how those things always feel the same. The same songs, same faces, same words, same coffee. Everybody is so different from everyone else, but when they die people say the same stuff that they said about all the other dead people. They were so nice. They had a great smile. They loved to have fun. Their families will miss them. *And it's all true. But when a girl dies and everyone goes on and on saying the same basic things about what a good and kind person she was, it makes you wonder how much anyone knows or cares about anyone else. Like ... PAY ATTENTION! If it had been me that died, the only thing different would be the pictures on the wall. Dying should mean something. It shouldn't be the same no matter who you are or what you do. It should be personal.*

Like with Destiny, people should have been losing it about WHY. I was in the same school with her for my whole life and we lived super close. I probably saw her just about every day even if we didn't really talk. How could I not know? I think about dying all the time, no matter how hard I try to clutter my brain with other things. What if I had really talked to her instead of wasting time feeling alone and ignored? We could have taken care of each other. Before Shane and I were together I used to bug her for information about the kinds of things that Shane likes so I would have stuff to talk to him about. But maybe if I had taken a second to get over myself and really look at her, I would have seen a version of myself looking back. Or maybe that's exactly what I did see and I couldn't look away fast enough. Maybe.

One time Destiny asked me what it felt like to be pretty. She was kind of goth and sarcastic a lot, but this time she wasn't. She asked like she really wanted to know. I told her not to be stupid and I said, I'm not any prettier than you are. *We both knew that was bullshit. She wasn't ugly or anything, but people can be assholes about heavier girls with bad skin. She didn't laugh much, but when she did, it was the nicest, most surprising sound. It made me feel lucky, like she had picked me alone to hear it.*

I keep trying to write something for her but I haven't figured it out yet. Usually poems come easier than anything else, but this time it's different. This is as far as I got:

Dead girls don't need your
love
Dead girls don't need you
to listen
Dead girls don't need your
help
Not anymore

It's messed to be jealous of a dead girl
I know that
But dead girls can't talk and dead girls can't dream
No one can hurt them

CHAPTER FOUR

When Shane arrives home from the memorial the house is still. He could go back to Destiny's room to make sure Jackie is home, but why bother. She hasn't left in weeks—she's not going anywhere now. Shane pulls a box of no-name cereal from the cupboard and shakes them into a bowl. The O's make soft sounds when they hit the milk.

"Mom!" No answer. "Do you want some cereal?"

Destiny's bed creaks softly under his mother's weight, but no other sound comes from the room.

Shane holds his breath and hopes for the sound of shuffling footsteps that would tell him she is coming out. When she hasn't emerged a few minutes later, he sets the bowl of cereal outside Destiny's door. It'll be empty by the end of the day.

Shane upends the milk carton into his bowl, but the dribble that comes out isn't even enough to drown a tick. All that's left in the fridge is the dregs of a tub of yogurt and a dried-up heel of bologna loosely wrapped in plastic. He pops open the tub of yogurt. Pinkish mold bubbles on the surface and creeps up the side of the container.

*

Janice's store is pretty much the only place to buy anything on the rez. Most people do a big grocery shop at Walmart or somewhere like that when they drive down to Brickport, but Shane doesn't have a car, and he's eager to get the nasty taste of that yogurt out of his mouth. Janice's will have to do. When he gets to the door, Shane runs into Roberta, who is juggling a plastic bag full of groceries, a hot coffee, and her cell phone, all while trying to put her sunglasses on.

"Hey, Berta."

Roberta looks up and smiles. "Get in here, kid." She wraps him in a hug. "That was tough today. You okay?"

Shane nods.

"I wanted to talk to you about your school funding at the memorial, but it didn't seem appropriate."

"Okay."

"It doesn't look like you're going to get funded this year."

"What? Why not?"

"When you were born, you were registered as a member on your dad's rez. After he died, nobody changed you over here, so you're technically still on the rolls at Eagle Creek. But Eagle Creek won't fund you because you've never lived there. And they've already allocated their budget for student support."

"Can't you just get me transferred to the band here?"

"We can work together on it, but they won't be looking at education funding again until next year. I was going through back channels to get it sorted out for you, but then Destiny died and … there hasn't been a good time to talk."

This is exactly the kind of bullshit that makes him want to get out of here. It seems like people are always saying, *There is help out there but not for you, not right now.* When he goes online and sees how the rest of the country lives, it feels like Indians are the only people without options or choices. Pinned down under the thumb of the government with a whole agency determining where they live, how much money they have access to, how they can develop their land, who belongs to the community, and who doesn't. A whole bureaucracy set up to tell Anishinaabe people who they are and what they can be. An army of smiling people in government offices and band offices saying "we want to help!" and then explaining why they can't.

"The first deposit for tuition and housing is due in a few weeks," Roberta says.

Shane squints past her, as though he's trying to make out a shape in the distance. "That's the first two grand?"

Roberta nods. "Sorry it's not better news. Think your mom can swing it?"

Roberta must know his mom hasn't got any money. The only reason she's asking is because she's out of answers and she's hoping Shane has one.

"You could look into a loan," Roberta suggests.

Roberta knows she's scraping the bottom of the barrel. Education is a right granted by the treaties between The Anishinaabek of Treaty 3 and the Canadian government. There aren't a lot of kids willing to go twenty grand in debt a year just to get something that the government is supposed to guarantee in exchange for taking pretty much all of the land and natural resources and exploiting them at a massive profit for generations.

"Think about it, okay?" Roberta says. "We'll start processing your band membership transfer now."

"I should get going," Shane says.

"Can you let me know if I need to ask the university to delay your admission a year?"

They keep talking, but Shane isn't paying attention anymore. Roberta wants so badly for him to be fine that she'll never notice that he's checked out.

When there's a gap in the conversation, Shane opens the door of the store and steps inside, feeling the itch of Roberta's gaze between his shoulder blades. Above him, dusty fluorescent lights hang from the beige popcorn ceiling. Janice's store has all the charm of a cardboard box. Shane nods at Ashley, who squints her eyes at him from behind the cash register. He doesn't remember when she got so hard. Back when they were kids, she was one of those bright lights that would never stop smiling. Her humor has survived in the form of a forked tongue that can praise you and cut you down in a single lash. Shane pulls a carton of milk, a box of cereal, a loaf of white bread, and some eggs from the shelves.

Ashley rings Shane's purchases through the till without looking up. Janice, the store manager, waves Shane over to her. Everything about Janice—her hair, mouth, hips—all of it droops low down, as though gravity has a stronger effect on her than it does on other people. Maybe it does. Nothing else in life is handed out equally.

"Hey, College. How's your mom?" Janice asks.

"She's okay."

"I still got the stuff for you guys' roof out back, hey?"

"My uncle Pete's gonna pick it up, I think."

"He gonna pay for it too?"

Ashley rolls her head to one side. "Shane, your total's $28.97." Shane glances apologetically at Janice and escapes back to the till, grabbing a credit card from his wallet.

Janice eyes him steadily. "It's close to seven grand. I can't just sit on it all summer. You guys gotta pay."

Shane nods. "I know. I'll see what Uncle Pete says." Shane picks up his grocery bags and leaves the store before Janice can ask any more questions.

A few months ago they had a particularly bad stretch of storms. One night when Shane and Destiny were home alone, they noticed that what had started as a tiny brown patch on the ceiling had spread to both sides of the wall. It was bulging like the belly of a pregnant moose. Shane dared Destiny to poke it with the tip of her fishing rod. Destiny could never resist a dare, especially one from her brother, so she dashed out of the room and dragged her rod, clattering, out of the cupboard. *Do it!* Shane laughed.

Destiny lifted the rod up to the ceiling and pushed, ever so gently. The water must have soaked that drywall pretty good, because her rod pushed through it like a fork through mashed potatoes. And the stinking water that dribbled out was as brown and thick as gravy. Destiny shrieked and jumped away, but not before some of it landed in her hair and ran down her neck. They thought it was hilarious at first, but over time the hole in the ceiling grew; the hole in the roof must have been getting worse too, because the amount of water coming through the ceiling increased with every rainfall. Lately, tendrils of black mold have been shooting out from the edges of the hole like the roots of a hungry vine cracking open a clay pot.

When Shane and Destiny first asked about fixing it, Jackie pursed her lips and said, *If it bugs you, don't look up.* They all laughed and pretended to forget about it for a while longer. And it worked for a while, but the problem grew and eventually Jackie ordered a bunch of construction materials from the store. Pete and some buddies were supposed to help rebuild the roof and re-shingle it when the time came, but he said without materials nothing could begin. Jackie had planned to pay with the bit of money she had saved up, but between her not going to work and Destiny's funeral, that was pretty much gone. In the meantime, the house was rotting from the inside out.

*

Shane hurries home from the store. It's getting late. The lake is gray with flashes of white. The wind kisses the top of a wave, making it flutter like a tuft of hair blown out of place. Stretched-out plastic grocery bags hang from Shane's hands, threatening to burst. He pries the screen door open with his foot and pushes against the inside door of the house. The lights are off, but enough afternoon sunlight comes in the kitchen window to guide him through the room.

The countertop is scattered haphazardly with sympathy cards, ignored bills, and unopened letters, which all probably say nicer versions of the same thing: *Sorry your sister is dead.* Shane wipes gritty crumbs off a stack of university course selection materials. Impossibly bright, confident faces of young students smile from the cover, gloating about the promises their lives hold. Above their sun-dappled hair, the pamphlet declares that these are *The Faces of the Future.* Shane buries the pamphlet deep in the random stack of mail, not quite silencing the call to freedom that tugs at him like the moon against the ocean.

He opens the door of the freezer and rearranges the containers of casseroles with condolence notes taped to the sides.

"Hey, Mom? Did you talk with Roberta about my deposit for school?" Shane listens for a response. Nothing. He leaves the rest of the groceries on the counter and walks down the hall toward the open door of Destiny's room.

"Janice was asking about the roofing stuff again too."

Shane pauses inside the door frame. It feels wrong to be in here. Destiny was always protective of her space, and it doesn't seem right that Jackie has claimed it as her own. Shane wonders if she would have camped out in his room if he had been the one who died. No, she wouldn't. It's different with mothers and daughters. Jackie never expected Shane to make his own bed, but his mom used to just lose it if Destiny went to school without making hers. When Shane asked his mom why she was so hard on Destiny, she said, *A mother's dreams for the future live in her son, but her spirit lives in her daughter.* Shane thought about that a lot after Destiny died. He can name the pieces of his mother that left with Destiny —the piece that loves the sun, the piece that laughs and teases, the piece that keeps watch over him—all of that's gone, and it may never come back. .

Shane steps toward the bed. Jackie's cheek is pressed into the familiar groove of her daughter's pillow, like a little girl taking a nap. He tries to picture his mother when she was young, and comes up empty. He has seen pictures of her unwrapping presents in front of a Christmas tree, but when he tries to remember the details, a gnarled vision comes instead: half woman and half child, with his mother's tangle of salt-and-pepper hair. Her grief-torn grown-up face transplanted onto her little-girl body in a candy cane dress.

Shane forces himself back to the present. To the room with his mother, asleep. "Mom?"

Jackie doesn't stir. Shane lifts a patchwork quilt from the wooden chair and opens it up wide. He feels Destiny enter the room as if his panic has called her to him. When he turns his head, she's on the other side of the bed, shaking her side of the blanket out by the corners, mirroring him. She's wearing the same ripped fishnet stockings and her eyes are sad. He wishes he could yell at her, "*This is all your fault!*" but he's afraid that would make her disappear and he would never see her again. So he stays quiet as they lift the quilt up high over their mother's fetal-curled body. It billows out and comes to rest over her hips, settling like a crane on the water. Something settles in him too, if only for a moment. Shane turns to smile at Destiny, but she's already gone.

Jackie lets out a long breath. Her body looks heavy under the quilt. Older. Shane picks up a stack of dirty dishes from beside Destiny's bed.

Jackie speaks without opening her eyes. "Close the door on your way out."

Maybe it shouldn't hurt that she has so little to say to him—he knows she's in pain—but it does. Shane balances a plate carefully on his arm and pulls the door softly behind him.

"Aanii!" Evie says.

Shane jerks his head around like a frightened deer. Evie is there by the back door, taking off her shoes. Nothing to be scared of. Shane tells himself to relax, but that terrified animal inside him won't stop running.

"Jesus—you scared me. I thought you were gone." Shane sets the dirty dishes with the others and starts the water.

"Better not use that guy's name like that."

"Why? You don't believe in that stuff."

"Still. Their spirits are powerful too."

Shane nods, more to placate her than anything else. When his mom and Evie are fighting, Jackie calls her a born-again Indian. She says Evie was a good Catholic girl for years after residential school, but when Indians got political in the '70s and '80s, she got drawn into the pan-Indian fad for "walking the red road" and never looked back. People called her a faker for a long time, but she stopped drinking, became fluent in the language, and learned their ceremonies from the few who still remembered. She's been teaching the songs, the language, sharing the culture ever since. If that's what a faker or a "pretendian" looks like, then he doesn't know what being a real Indian is. Broke-down cars, bingo, and sconedogs? He doesn't think so. There's not much left of the Catholic girl Evie once was, but she does get funny when people bring up Jesus.

Evie sighs heavily and leans against the counter, watching Shane scrub at some caked-on pasta sauce at the bottom of a bowl. "Why don't you let me take care of that?"

"I got it."

Evie uses her hip to nudge Shane away from the sink. "I know. You're doing real good. But let me do something useful. You want to help out later you can give my old feet a rub." Evie's eyes twinkle at him. "Neeeeeeee."

Shane laughs a little in spite of himself. He watches her rough brown hands moving carefully under the steaming water and wonders how she always makes him feel better without seeming to do anything.

"Don't you get tired of being around people who are sad all the time?" Shane asks.

"Even when we're sad, our people still laugh. You know that, right? And I'm there for the good stuff too. Don't worry—I make sure to get my fun in." Evie winks at him.

Shane laughs. She's a terror when she gets on her snow machine. People say she's basically blind, but it doesn't seem to slow her down, and if you ask Shane, she sees a lot more than most people.

"Why don't you get out of here for a bit tonight?" Evie says. "I'll stay with your mom. You don't do any fun stuff anymore."

"What should I do?"

"I'm sure you and that pretty girlfriend of yours will think of something."

CHAPTER FIVE

No matter what else is going on, Shane and his friends always start the night at Debbie's compound. That's where the booze is. The place is a ramshackle collection of buildings that have been put up over the last fifty or sixty years by a succession of uncles and cousins and reluctant brothers-in-law. The main little house was built first, by Debbie's grandpa, and the second building was added out back when he wanted to build a still. It didn't take long for Debbie's grandpa to start selling his hooch, and the family has been in the bootleg business ever since. No one much cares, except that some of their best clients are kids. But even so, most people were happy to turn a blind eye until Debbie got ambitious about fifteen years ago and started selling drugs. Nobody has done anything about it other than reporting her to the police, for all the good that does. They come around every once in a while and tell her to keep the noise under control, or warn her not to sell to kids, but that's as far as it goes. Something pretty serious would have to go down before they would step in.

Debbie watches over the whole area from behind a folding

card table on the porch. In the winter she moves the operation inside, but at the first sign of the thaw, and right up until the snow falls, Debbie can be found out on that porch with her shelves of liquor, ratty old fridges full of beer, and the safe at her feet. Somebody tried to make off with the safe once, but it was so heavy they couldn't even get it off the porch. All they did was make a mess of her shelves and give themselves a scare when Debbie got up to see what the fuss was. Not that she moved fast enough to see who it was. She just replaced it with a heavier one the next week.

When Shane steps onto the property, Debbie slants her eyes sideways at him without turning her head. That's classic; she's so shapeless, heavy, and hard that she looks more like a bag of cement than a real human woman. She's probably forty but with all that makeup it's hard to tell. It sits on her face like a spooky mask, smearing her features into something from the spirit world. Shane once got Ashley to try to picture Debbie on the toilet, but she couldn't. Ashley laughed for about ten minutes straight, calling out different normal human things that they couldn't imagine Debbie doing, like kissing or breastfeeding or trying to put in a contact lens.

"You bring me a coffee?" Debbie says.

Shane shows his empty hands. Debbie kisses her teeth and goes back to her Sudoku. Sometimes she won't let people buy from her until they go to the store and get her a coffee—three creams, three sugars. Most of her regulars stop at the store for a cup so that they don't get turned away; she's got them trained. Debbie is a lot of things, but she's not stupid.

Tara, Kyle, and Ashley are sitting around on a beat-up old couch that's been out in the middle of Debbie's compound since

Shane can remember. Kyle is next to Tara. He's leering as usual, but he probably thinks he's being charming. Who knows—Tara might even think he's charming. He's definitely the best-looking guy on the rez. Shane has to remind himself sometimes what a greasy shit he is, so he doesn't get a crush.

Kyle punches the air. "Colleeeeeege!"

Shane smiles a little. He's never sure how to interpret Kyle's attempts at friendship. "What's going on?"

Kyle puts his arm around Tara. "Me and your girl here were just chillin'. She looks good, hey? Shirt's a bit small though."

Ashley gives him cut-eye. "Better throw some of that my way if you wanna get some tonight."

Kyle puts a hand on Ashley's knee and nuzzles her neck. "You know I love you."

Tara glances down at her chest and zips up her green hoodie. "Oh hey—you guys hear that Annalise got knocked up?"

Ashley swivels around to Tara. "Nooooooo—really? Since when?"

Kyle spreads his legs and leans back. "Musta been some white guy from Brickport. Nobody 'round here'd touch that skank."

This whole conversation is bullshit, and they all know it. There's a new rumor about Annalise every week. She started as the butt of jokes when she arrived from Akwesasne when they were in kindergarten. With no parents or cousins on the rez—just an auntie that married into the community—and being the only Mohawk, it was never going to be easy for her. Not that Shane is innocent. The cruelest thing Shane has allowed himself to think after Destiny's suicide was that it should have been Annalise. At least with her no one would wonder why. *Of course the fat, bullied, lonely Mohawk girl killed herself.* With Destiny there wasn't anything specific to point to. Nothing obvious at least.

No one has said anything for a minute or so. Shane casts a quick glance around the group. It's weird that after a lifetime of knowing one another it can feel sometimes like they've only just met. Or maybe they know each other so well that there's nothing left to talk about. Drinking usually solves the problem, but not always.

"You guys got any drinks?" Shane asks. They all shake their heads. "Any money?"

Kyle laughs. "Nah."

Shane twists around to address Debbie. "Hey, Deb! How about cutting us a deal?"

"Why would I do that?"

Kyle leans forward. "C'mon, Auntie. We're family!"

Debbie snorts. "I know *you* got money. I pay you enough." Kyle flops back on the couch.

Shane turns back to the group. "Never mind—I got it. I'm gonna be leaving you Injuns in the dust once I start making money in the city anyways." A chorus of ooooooohs and laughter come back at him. This was clearly a stupid thing to say, since he and his mom are careening deeper into debt by the day, but sometimes you have to just say *fuck it* and go all out.

Ashley shoves Tara's shoulder. "You're gonna have to watch one of those college bitches don't run off with him. He's a prize, this one."

"I'm gonna be there with him so they won't get the chance."

Shane freezes, knowing Tara must be watching for a reaction after dropping that bomb. *She's coming with me? Who makes an announcement like that in front of a bunch of people without even being invited?*

"Awww … now you got a wife!" Kyle shouts. Shane gets up off the couch to keep from losing his shit.

Their voices follow him as he walks over to the fridges where Debbie is sitting.

"Girls like you never leave," Ashley says.

Kyle laughs. "They'll come back next year all whitewashed and just real snobby 'bout everything."

"Too late!" Ashley shrieks.

Shane calls back to Kyle. "And what about you? You graduated like four years ago. You just gonna keep sitting around on your auntie's couch jerking it all day?" Shane can tell that one struck a nerve, because Kyle stumbles a bit. "I— I'm gonna take over the family business!"

"HA! You'll need to learn how to count first!" Debbie snaps back. Everyone laughs. Debbie turns to Shane and winks. "Whaddaya want?"

"Vodka." Shane passes Debbie some cash. She flattens it carefully and tucks it into the heavy metal safe that sits beside her. Debbie gets up with a cracking of joints and shuffles to the fridges. Shane can't help but let his eyes be drawn to the memorial wall Debbie has set up behind the card table. There's a gaudy crucifix that she mounted near the ceiling with a photo collage of dead and missing community members pasted lovingly below. Car accidents, drownings, overdoses, suicides—the ones who died of natural causes didn't usually make it to Debbie's board, unless they were related to someone high up in her church. A wide ribbon above the crucifix says *Forever at Peace* in curling script. With a sickening lurch, Shane notices a school photo of Destiny mounted in the middle of the display. A centerpiece. His field of vision narrows, carving away the clutter of buildings and the other faces on the wall until all he can see is Destiny's eyes. *Is that the way Debbie always does it, with the most recently departed taking up the middle spot like some fucked-up version of employee of the month?* Shane claws through his memories but he can't recall who last occupied that place of honor.

There was one time when Shane was here at Debbie's compound about a year ago looking for Kyle, but no one was around. There were chains on the fridges to keep people from messing with them, but the scrapbook was still out. Shane had seen it before, but this was the only time he got a chance to sneak a look at it. When he opened the cover, he saw page after page of names, pictures, and obituaries. All the suicides, disappearances, and accidental deaths in the community for the last thirty years had been cataloged, starting with Debbie's brother. He fell through the ice one night in March, in a spot everyone, including him, knew was too thin to hold a man's weight. Some of the Catholics didn't want him in their graveyard, but Debbie wouldn't take no for an answer.

Now, while Debbie's back is turned, Shane opens up the scrapbook again. He knows what he's going to find there, and he knows it's going to make him feel worse, but he has to look anyway. Shane flips past decades of yellowed newsprint with notes in the margins, stories and photos of people gone before their time. Tragedy after tragedy. When he gets to the last page, Destiny's face is there smiling back at him. Debbie has the funeral program pasted at the back of the book with a handwritten note: *suicide, hanging.* When Shane looks up, Debbie is watching. She smiles, showing a bit of lipstick on her teeth. "It's a nice picture, isn't it?"

Shane scans her features for a sign that she's trying to be cruel or kind. But maybe it's neither. Maybe she's just stating a fact. "Yeah, it is nice," he says lamely.

*

Shane and the others take off from the compound with the 40 of vodka in hand, looking like a bunch of kids let out from school early. Once they get some distance from Debbie's they stop and huddle in the middle of the road. They each hold out their red plastic cup for Shane to fill. An amber glow from the security light at Janice's store warms their faces.

"'Bout time we got our drink on," grumbles Kyle.

"Is that you saying thanks?" Shane fills his cup, then moves on to fill the others'.

They take a few sips, enough to keep from spilling while they walk, then set off toward the lake. The vodka loosens their tongues and gives them permission to have the kind of fun that, as they get older, seems impossible to do without a little help. When they turn the corner, laughing, David is walking ahead of them.

Kyle points with his lips and calls out, "That kid is such a fag."

Ashley slaps Kyle's shoulder playfully. "Don't say that. It makes you sound like a prick!"

"I don't care."

David crosses to the other side of the street, obviously trying to get away from them. Shane shakes his head. *As if you can avoid anyone in a place this small.*

Kyle shouts out, "What, me and Shane aren't your type, medicine man!?" Kyle laughs at his own joke, but no one else does. They know that encouraging him inevitably leads to bigger problems. Shane keeps his eyes on his feet, silently willing Kyle to stop.

"No, seriously, you're hurting my feelings now!" Kyle yells.

David walks a little faster. "Don't be an asshole," Shane says. "He was Destiny's best friend." Kyle looks back at Shane like he's trying to figure out whether he wants to go after him or David. But Shane is Kyle's booze ticket for the night, so he's safe.

"It's true, Kyle. He was," Tara says.

Shane watches David's hunched shoulders up ahead. Until now, he's been careful not to spend time with David in public. But it's possible that their shared grief over Destiny's death might be enough to justify the two of them hanging out. People might still talk, but they'd have an excuse. Shane breaks eye contact with Kyle. "Back in a sec."

Shane jogs up behind David. "Hey!" Shane calls.

David's head jerks around, wide-eyed. "Oh shit—it's just you."

"Sorry—did I scare you?" David shrugs. "Why don't you walk with us for a bit?"

David eyes the others suspiciously. "Where?"

"Wherever."

Kyle calls out in a high-pitched, lisping voice, "Daveeeeey. I won't bite, Daveeeey!"

David glances over his shoulder at Kyle. "Nah, I'm just gonna head home."

"C'mon. It'll be fun."

"I seriously doubt that."

Shane tries to pass David his cup, but he pushes it away. Shane doesn't have the patience to keep this up. "What's wrong with you?"

David thumbs the zipper of his hoodie uncertainly. "You totally ignored me at the memorial."

"I thought you wanted to play it cool when we're out."

"Yeah. But you were like, glued to Tara though."

"I wouldn't still be with her if you didn't want it that way."

David frowns. Shane knows he's messing this up, but he honestly has no idea what David wants most of the time. Sometimes what they have feels crazy intense, like they're the only people on the planet who have ever really *seen* each other. But other times it's like this.

They grew up together, but they never really hung out much until David and Destiny became really close a year and a half ago. It started with Shane hanging out with David and Destiny from time to time, playing video games or wandering around in the bush. Shane had heard a rumor that David was gay, and he didn't know if it was true, but the idea sparked something in him. He definitely didn't think of himself as gay. But he didn't really know what he was or when you were supposed to figure it out for sure. Maybe he didn't need a label. All the available words felt dirty or wrong somehow. When he let his mind go there, the idea of kissing a mouth with stubble around it made him hard in about five seconds. But a bit of breeze while walking around in sweatpants could do the same thing so he didn't really know if it was David he was attracted to or men in general, or just the novelty of it.

The first time something happened between him and David was at Shane's house one night when David was sleeping over.

Destiny had already gone to bed, and David was supposed to be sleeping in the living room. A little after midnight, Shane heard a tap at his door, and then it opened quietly.

"You awake?" David asked.

"Yeah."

David closed the door behind him and came toward the bed. "I couldn't sleep, and Destiny's right out of it, so … is it okay I'm here?"

"Yeah. Sure. No problem."

"Thanks."

"You can sit down here if you want." Shane pulled himself up awkwardly as David settled on the blanket beside him. Shane drew the blankets a little more tightly around his waist, excruciatingly aware that he was naked under the covers. Shane looked at David, taking in every tic and signal he might be giving with his body language, searching David's face for an objection, a threat, or an invitation.

"The couch is kind of uncomfortable. I think I'm too tall for it now."

"Oh. Yeah?" Shane asked, appalled at his inability to string together a group of words more than one or two syllables long.

"Do you think I could sleep here? I'll be out before your mom and Destiny are up, I promise."

Shane panicked. He had no idea what to say. "Uhhh … I would but I'm sleeping naked."

"That's okay." David stood up and pulled off his T-shirt. Shane admired the soft curve of David's spine in the moonlight for a moment before he realized that David was pulling off his underwear too.

Holy shit. What's going on?

Shane caught a brief glimpse of David's erection before he slid into bed and it disappeared beneath the covers. David turned so that he and Shane were face-to-face, but not touching. Shane's mind dashed through the sequence of events since David had come into the room, searching for any indication that he was wrong about what he thought was going on here. He felt the heat from David pulsing toward him like waves lapping at the shore.

From that night on, David slept over at Shane and Destiny's house a lot. Shane hung out with his other friends as much as possible, keeping his distance from David during school. He was smart. He had lots of friends and a great girlfriend, but it didn't feel like he was really living until after midnight, alone in his bedroom with David. It wasn't right that he would have to give up his whole life here to build something with David, but that's what it would take. As far as he knew, there had never been any couples like them on the rez. He was ready to do it, though. He was ready to walk away from it all and start something new, but David wouldn't let him.

Now with Destiny gone, there are no more excuses for them to see each other. As far as anyone knows, they aren't even friends, so the endless tangled-up nights in Shane's bedroom are a thing of the past. When they can get together, one of them always has his eye on the door, terrified of being discovered. Eventually they always find a way to lose themselves in the moment, but the pleasure of burying their grief in each other's bodies never lasts long. Walking home alone, Shane always feels worse than he did before. These days, any kind of pleasure feels wrong.

*

"You drinking with us or what?" Ashley asks, stone-faced. Kyle and Tara trail behind her. It looks like their red cups are nearly empty.

"Of course he is," Shane says.

This time, when Shane passes his drink to David, he takes it.

"I thought medicine men didn't drink," Kyle sneers.

"Priests aren't supposed to touch little boys either, and we all know how that worked out." David winks and takes a sip of vodka.

Huh huh huh huh! Ashley's low belly laugh gathers momentum until everyone joins in. It's impossible not to laugh when Ashley is laughing. Thank god she laughs a lot—they've needed it lately.

"What did you say to me?"

David throws him a look that says, *You heard me*, then tosses his head back and downs Shane's drink in one go.

That gets Ashley going again, which sets the others off. "Huh, huh, huh, aaiiieeeeeeeee ha ha ha ha ha!!!!!!" Ashley tries to catch her breath. "Fuckin' medicine man! Aaaaiiieeeeeeeeee hahahaha!" Kyle shakes his head and shoves his hands in his pockets, sulking. One by one, each of them runs out of laughter, until all they can hear is the whine of unseen insects.

"So, medicine man, is your grandma still talking to ghosts and shit?" Kyle smiles to make it seem like he's not still pissed.

Shane doesn't buy it. "Shut up, Kyle, you don't know what you're talking about."

Kyle smirks. "I'm just sayin'. It's not my problem they don't believe in god."

"So? I don't believe in god either." Ashley laughs.

Kyle grabs a handful of her ass. "Yeah, but we already know you're going to hell."

"If I do it's your fault!" Ashley gives Kyle a shove, but Shane can just tell she's loving her life right now. When Ashley and Kyle first got together, Shane bet Tara that they wouldn't last more than a week after Kyle started having sex with Ashley. But here they are more than a year later. Kyle's always chasing other girls, but as long as it's kept out of Ashley's face she seems happy enough with the crumbs he gives her.

David looks like he's been holding his breath for the last minute or so. Shane makes a mental note to get better at predicting and avoiding moments like these, when the two sides of his life collide.

"The spirits are real," David says. "Ask the old people."

"Which old people? My old people tell me your spirits are just the devil, so …" Kyle catches a look between Shane and David. "What do your old people say about smoking pole? Your spirits like to watch that?"

Shane stops walking. "Jesus Christ. Can both of you just shut up? Nobody wants to hear you argue about whose fairy tales are better."

Tara and Ashley giggle uncomfortably. Shane feels David pulling away, like air rushing out of a balloon.

Ashley gasps and her eyes widen like a bad actress in a horror movie. "Oh god … I can feel it now!"

"Feel what?" Kyle asks.

"The spirits. They're … they're gonna get us!" Ashley's voice trembles, trying to make her bubbling laughter seem like a sob.

Tara grabs Ashley's wrist and bugs her eyes out. "Oh shiiiit, I can feel it too!"

"Run!" Tara takes off running, yanking Ashley by the sleeve. Ashley yelps and allows herself to be dragged, cackling with laughter, behind her. Kyle shakes his head and jogs after them, following the girls down a path to the beach. Shane and David watch them go. Their voices fade into the night, already sounding like a memory of laughter.

Shane cranes his neck behind him. The road is empty. He tentatively reaches out and hooks David's pinkie with his finger. It's awkward, as if by touching him he's actually increased the distance between them. David jerks his hand away and puts it in his pocket where Shane can't reach it. So much for romance.

CHAPTER SIX

Back at home. Hiding in my room waiting for Shane to text.
I lost track of him and David after we ran to the beach.
I kept thinking they were behind us but they must have
thought we were going someplace else because they never
showed up. I hate being around Kyle without Shane. As soon
as there's a woman without a boyfriend he's all over her like
a dog marking his territory. Seriously. I swear he'd spray me
with pee and claim me as his own if he could get away with
it. He'd do the same with half of the girls around here if he
could. He didn't even care that Ashley was there. He took
every chance he could to tuck a bit of hair behind my ear or
to put his arms around me to "help me up" off the ground.
Creep. Ashley finally shoved him off when he tried to kiss
me. He said he was just fooling around but … whatever.

Speaking of creeps, Dad is on the prowl again. I came
in to find him with some cheap piece from Brickport or

*somewhere. He tried to get me to hang out, but I've been
down that road. He gets a few drinks in and suddenly
his hands do whatever they want to without thinking,
apparently. It's partly my fault. When I was younger I let it
happen because I thought it was normal. But I can spot the
signs better now and mostly avoid him when he's like that.*

*I started to write another poem on my way home but I can
hardly remember it now.*

> *Battle-worn girls drum*
> *Down the winter road*
> *Calluses cracked open with blood and dirt.*
> *We climb*
> *Rattles clattering over*
> *Potholes and fallen trees*
> *Fallen sisters in our path.*
>
> *They say the trail's been blazed.*
> Ha. Funny. Tell me another one.
> *Torched, more like.*
> *Ashes and tears make*
> *Shitty war paint*
>
> *No matter.*
> *Our feet keep moving.*
> *Eyes peeled for signs of spring*
> *Shoots of fireweed*
> *From cold embers.*

Ashley always bugs me about what I'm writing. I tell her it's just something to pass the time, but we both know that's a lie. When I reach out for a word and put it in my book, I become more solid. Like I've been a ghost for my whole life but now, with a pen in my hand, I might be able to write myself into existence. Into someone worth seeing, worth being, worth taking care of. Maybe one day I'll feel like I'm finally myself and can put my pen down.

CHAPTER SEVEN

The sky and the water glitter endlessly in the moonlight. Shane and David pick their way down to the unlit point by looking for the narrow band of rocks and shadow, the only place that doesn't sparkle with silver stars and their jittery reflections. Wind rushes through the shoulder-high grass, telling stories in a language Shane wishes he could understand. Evie and the elders say people have to listen to the voices of the four-legged people, the rock people, and the plant people. Hearing that makes the hairs on his neck stand up, but he stops short of believing it's real. Last year, Shane told Mr. Kolasky what Evie said about talking to animals. Kolasky pushed his glasses up on his beak and scrutinized Shane's face, trying to gauge how serious he was. Science teachers can't stand to be teased. After a moment, Mr. Kolasky told Shane that Evie was probably speaking more metaphorically than literally. He said that there are many ways to "talk" to the plants and animals, and scientific study is probably the most effective way. When Shane told Evie what Mr. Kolasky had said, she couldn't stop laughing all night.

*

Shane looks over at the glossy sliver of David's profile. Even though there's no one around to see, he's got his shoulders pulled back and head held high, carrying himself proud and strong, like a goddamn prince in the starlight. Shane wonders if that posture comes from having a sense of responsibility and purpose in the world, or if it's something he was just born with. It seems at odds with his fear of being public with Shane, but if the thing that's making him strong is his connection to the teachings and the cultural people, and that's what he stands to lose, it makes sense. Everyone is afraid of something. Shane used to be afraid. Now he's just tired.

David turns to Shane with a frown. "Don't say that shit to me again. Our culture isn't a fairy tale."

"I'm sorry. I didn't mean it like that."

"Yes, you did." David isn't looking at him.

He's right. Some days Shane has a hard time separating elders talking about their spirits and medicine from Christians talking about drinking the blood of Christ and praying to the holy ghost. But then he steps into the sun and feels the buzz of something in the ground and the air, a kind of hum that's in his body and in the mud and the water, a whisper of knowing that his spirit is home. It's in the kiss of the waves on his thighs in summer, the thundering of wings overhead in a storm. The elders may not be right about everything, but there is something in this place that can't be explained with language. Words fail every time.

The boys arrive at their secret spot, a place on the point where a cluster of trees and underbrush block them from being seen by anyone onshore or around the powwow grounds. Based on how things are going, Shane isn't sure how long David will want to stay. It's been a week since they were alone together. It feels like every cell in his body is singing out for David to touch him. Shane reaches out for David's hand. "I'm sorry."

David doesn't pull away this time. Shane lifts David's arm and drapes it around his shoulders, positioning him so they stand in a loose embrace.

"I didn't hug you."

"Yeah, but you wanted to." Shane closes his eyes, savoring the warmth and weight of him. David doesn't pull away, but doesn't give in either. Shane presses his lips against David's mouth and holds there, breathing him in. The anger in David's lips melts away. Shane runs his hand under David's shirt. The skin of his torso is smooth like sun-warmed sandstone. David presses against him harder. Shane fingers one of David's rubbery blueberry nipples. David jumps back like he's been smacked and pulls down his shirt.

"We can't. Someone might see."

"There's barely enough light for me to see you, let alone someone across the lake."

"Still. At least at your place we could lock the door."

Shane sighs. He knows better than to push it. If it was up to him, they would have just said fuck it and come out months ago. He'll be gone soon anyway. *Mind over matter: those that matter don't mind and those that mind don't matter.*

David's arms are wrapped tightly around himself. "You cold?" Shane asks.

David shrugs. "Maybe we should go."

"Let me start a fire." Shane sets to work finding dead branches and driftwood in the dark. He can't tell how much his eyes can actually see and how much it's instinct that guides him to the solid-seeming areas of darkness to find what he's looking for. Shane tosses each piece he finds into a pile near David's feet.

"This is boring," David says.

"You could help."

David resists for a moment, then picks up a rock and places it beside another on the ground. Shane watches him dip in and out of the moonlight, gathering stones and setting them in a circle to form a fire pit. Shane sorts through a pile of debris and pulls out the smallest sticks and leaves. He crouches down on his knees beside the rocks and presses the small dry bits into a loose ball. He can feel David's eyes on his back. *Am I doing it wrong?* Shane hates it when he feels like a bad Indian.

"You doing it log-cabin or tipi style?"

"Guess." Shane surrounds the pile with sticks, resting the top ends against one another.

David passes him a lighter and drags a log up from the shoreline for something to sit on. Shane touches the flame to the dry summer leaves. It smolders there like it's trying to decide what to do and then catches with a flare that trickles through the sticks like water between his fingers. Watching the fire grow, Shane feels the presence of his ancestors like an echo behind him. Generations that crouched near the flames and warmed their palms, one after the other for tens of thousands of years. He wonders if white people ever feel something like that or if it's just Indians who feel their past and present breathing into each other.

"That was fun, hanging out with you and everyone else," Shane says. "That never happens."

"Was it?" David asks.

Shane shrugs. "I don't know. I guess. I was just saying." Shane watches the flames travel from the small sticks to the larger pieces of driftwood.

David speaks without looking at him. "The cops should shut Debbie's place down. She shouldn't be selling that stuff to kids. Everybody knows she does it too."

"That's never gonna happen."

A twig snaps, sending red sparks scattering into the sky. Shane shivers a little. Summer nights should be warmer than this. His mom used to get after him about wearing more layers when he went out, but he never listened.

"I was surprised you invited me out," David says quietly. "I saw you with those guys and I thought you would walk past like you didn't know me."

"Do you wish I had?" Shane looks up. David's mouth twitches like he's holding back a smile. That's good enough for Shane. "You slammed that 40 pretty good," Shane says. "I wasn't expecting that."

"Yeah, that was dumb. I feel like shit."

Shane looks at David's face in the firelight and smiles, a little goofy.

David blinks at him. "What?"

"Nothing." Shane wonders if this might be the right time to give him the guidebook. He's been carrying it around since before Destiny died, waiting for the right moment, but he always comes up with some excuse, some reason he should wait a little while longer. Shane rummages around in his backpack and pulls the book out. It's a tourist guide to the city of Toronto.

"I, uh … I've been carrying this around for a while. I keep

forgetting to give it to you." Shane passes it to David. David takes the book and opens it up to the glossy section of photos in the middle. One of the first pictures is a shirtless muscly guy with a water gun in his hands, surrounded by drag queens.

David quickly flips the page.

"Yeah, that's … there's other stuff too," Shane says. "There's a Native center where they do language classes and hold ceremonies, and there's a gay street with bars and bookstores and …" Shane can't believe he's about to say this. "I was thinking you could come with me."

David snaps the book shut and fixes his eyes on the flames.

"What do you think?" Shane asks.

"I don't get why you even want to go there."

"School. I want to learn how people put cities together. We can barely get a road paved or make sure we've got clean water year-round. It doesn't have to be like that. I'm sick of people complaining that shit isn't getting done. I want to be the one who learns how to fix this place and does it."

"You could go to a college nearby though."

Shane shakes his head. "Nah. Not even. Why would I go to some hick school in the middle of nowhere when I can go to the best school in the country?"

"They probably use the same books." David shrugs. "I just don't think that's the real reason you want to leave."

Shane pokes the fire. "I know how things'll go if I stay here. It's bullshit. What am I supposed to even do with my life here?" Shane glances at David. He's impossible to read. "I just wanna go where I can be with you and we can just do whatever we want. Be anything we want. You know?"

"I already know what I want to be. I don't need to go anywhere."

"Think people here are going to let you be who you want to be?"

David avoids Shane's eyes. "My *nookomis* and the elders have been teaching me a lot of things ..."

"So?"

"They say I can do something good here. They say I can make changes."

Shane leans back. "People tell me that all the time. They literally say that to everybody."

"Maybe it's true."

Shane snickers and shakes his head. "If you believe that ... I don't know what to tell you."

"Well, if the best you can do is run away ... I feel sorry for you." David looks down into the fire. A breeze pushes the smoke to the other side of the point.

He steals a look at David out of the corner of his eye. "You're so fucking stupid sometimes."

David's head snaps up. "Don't call me stupid. It's not stupid to want to stay here."

The fire snaps. Tiny embers tumble out around their feet. Shane nudges them back with the toe of his shoe. "So what if I want a chance to see what's out there, use my brain, maybe feel what it's like to introduce you to people as my boyfriend? Don't you ever wanna get out of here?"

David frowns. "Not really."

"So once I leave the rez, you're never gonna have sex. Never be with anyone again?"

David speaks softly. "I don't know. Why can't it just be between us? It has nothing to do with anyone else."

Shane isn't buying it. "And what about when all those traditional people find out you like dick? You think they're gonna let some fag teach them the culture? Good luck with that one." Shane is being mean, but his pride won't let him backtrack. Better to keep pushing until something breaks.

David slowly gets up and walks from the fire.

"What are you doing?" Shane asks.

"If you want a punching bag, go find your girlfriend." David hitches his bag over one shoulder and sets off in the darkness, heading toward the road. The moonlight leaches the color from David's skin as he moves farther away from the rusty firelight. Shane's eyes strain to pick his shape from the shadows, believing that as long as he can see him, there is a possibility that he might come back. By the time David reaches the base of the point, his body has faded into a lone gray smudge moving between the branches. Shane tells himself to call out after him, to explain that he understands; he wants to make things better too.

But it's harder than just wanting to make a difference. You have to have something to contribute. And right now it's all Shane can do to keep his own head above water while he takes care of his mom and tries to keep Tara and David happy. He loves both of them, but it isn't the same. He gets a cramp in his guts when he imagines breaking up with Tara. He pictures them doing things like going camping or playing with their dog or cooking at an apartment in the city. He can imagine that stuff with David too, but every time he thinks of him, those everyday thoughts are overshadowed by memories of their skin pressed together, the taste of sweat, and the feeling that they are more than right for each other—they are already part of each other. The first time they tried to fool around after Destiny died, they had to stop because they were crying too much. It felt gross and somehow weak to be tearing off their clothes when all they could think of was the ragged hole in their lives where Destiny used to be. They held each other for hours, not fooling around but not willing to go anywhere where their bodies couldn't touch.

Shane squints hard, willing the night to roll away like mist so he can see David again, even for a moment. Shane promises himself that he will count to five and then go after him.

One ... two ... three ... four ... five ...

Nope.

Shane closes his eyes. He pictures himself walking to the trees, where David would be waiting for him. Shane would apologize for all the things he said. David would forgive him without question.

I love you, Shane would say. Neither of them has said it yet, but he is pretty sure both of them feel the same way. It seems like one of those things where, once you say it, you can't take it back again. Like saying those words will create new life. Life with tissues and ligaments and a beating heart that wasn't there before. It's too real, maybe. So they end up in a game of chicken, with each of them hoping the other will say it first.

The fire at his feet has gone to ash, but there's heat in it still. Shane's phone buzzes. Shane unlocks the screen, hoping David sent some cute message to make him feel okay again. It's Tara: *Where R U?* Shane shoves his phone in his pocket without answering. The light glows like a firefly in his pocket.

CHAPTER EIGHT

Gravel crackles under the soles of Shane's shoes. Cold TV light pulses behind the curtains of the houses along the road. His phone buzzes with another message from Tara: *Come to my place. Dad's being gross again.*

Shane texts back: *It's late.*

Tara: *You know what he's like. I shouldn't have to ask.*

That hits Shane hard. She isn't wrong. They never talk about it, but he knows.

When Shane was over last week, Tara grabbed a beer out of the fridge for her dad, Glen. She bent over to reach inside, and Glen asked, *What you been eating to get that big ass? You got a booty like a black girl.* Tara stood up and pulled her T-shirt down. Glen let out a ragged laugh and winked at Shane. *I bet you like that, eh?* Shane couldn't imagine a response that wouldn't make Tara mad, or seem weirdly sexual in front of Glen. It was one of those panicky moments when Shane's mind spun out of control trying to figure out if it felt messed up because he wasn't like other teenage guys, or if it would just be messed up no matter who or what he was. Tara walked back to the living room and handed her dad the beer.

I always liked a flat bannock-butt better, Glen said. *But I guess if I was your age I'd wanna hit that too.* Shane responded with a half laugh and silence, hoping Glen would let it drop. There wasn't much else to do.

Glen will never get into any serious trouble for talking nasty to Tara, no matter how much it makes Shane feel like bashing Glen's head in. Talk is talk. But Shane has seen how scared Tara gets sometimes. He's seen the chair she tucks under her bedroom door to keep Glen and his friends out during the night. So Shane tried to have Tara over to his place as much as possible. His mom would never let her stay over because she said she's "not ready to be a grandma yet." And Shane goes over there when he can, but it's never enough. He knows Tara needs him, but he sometimes wonders if she uses her dad's behavior to trick Shane into spending more time with her. But even if that's true, does it matter?

Tara's chipped blue trailer is crouched low in the patchy grass, like a big cat ready to pounce. Faint light peeks between her curtains. As he gets closer, Shane feels the throb of Glen's subwoofer, cranked to max in the living room. There's no way he's going to risk a run-in with Tara's dad at this time of night, so Shane drags a plastic bucket from the yard up to Tara's window and climbs on top. Through the curtain, Shane can see that Tara's face is puffy from crying. A collection of her old stuffed animals is piled on the dresser and all the notes that Shane has passed her in class are taped to the walls. Shane knocks on the glass lightly. Tara's eyes dart to the window, panicked for a split second before she realizes it must be Shane.

Tara cautiously slides the window open. "It's about time."

"Come on, help me in." Shane reaches his hand out, and Tara uses her bodyweight to try to pull him in through the window. "Ow! Jesus Christ—I didn't say tear my arm off!"

Tara laughs and puts her finger up to her lips. "Shh!"

"Okay, just hold me steady. Don't pull." Tara hangs on, and Shane drags himself through the window awkwardly, kicking his legs out to shimmy inside. Shane falls to the floor with a heavy thud.

"Are you okay?"

"Yeah."

Shane pulls himself up so that he's sitting on the floor. Tara eyes him carefully as though she's not sure if she wants to know where he has been all night.

"Aren't you gonna kiss me?" she asks.

Shane's eyebrows jump up. "Oh yeah." He leans in and kisses Tara beside her mouth.

"So where were you?" she asks.

"You ran away," Shane reminds her.

"I was calling for you."

"I didn't hear anything." Shane pulls himself up high enough to flop into bed beside her. Tara reaches out and strokes his forehead. Shane's eyes close automatically. What they have feels old, like people who have been together so long that the touch of the other is like family. Love without fire.

"Tired?" Tara asks.

Shane slides down on the bed and curls into her.

She tries again. "Did you hear me earlier when I said I was coming to Toronto with you?"

Shane keeps his eyes closed. Is it believable that he might have fallen asleep this fast?

"Shane?" Tara shakes his shoulder gently.

She's not going to let this one go. He buys more time by pulling Tara into a long kiss. When in doubt, make out. *God, how is it that she always tastes like strawberry candy?* Shane runs his hand down her brushed-cotton panties. The fine muscles in her legs wave under his fingers like a school of minnows. In a single move, Tara pulls off her shirt. He can never get used to seeing her without her top on. It feels creepy and private, like watching someone pick their nose.

"You're bad," Shane says.

Tara lets her hand slide down his chest. "Everyone already thinks we're fucking."

"How do you know?"

"Ashley teases me sometimes. They just assume."

"You don't tell them we're not?"

Tara shrugs. "It's kind of embarrassing."

"Well, I don't wanna knock you up and get stuck here." It sounded like a joke in his head, but it might have been too true to be funny.

Tara sighs. "Could be worse."

He feels the creep of her hand moving under his waistband. Shane turns to his side. "I better get home. I've got to get up early and clean. The house is gross."

"She shouldn't still be making you do everything. It's been a couple months already."

"Six weeks."

"Still. Don't you get tired of being good? It wasn't your fault."

Tara touches his hair. Shane swats her hand away, but then regrets it. She didn't do anything wrong. She deserves better. He pulls her in, spooning her from behind. It feels intimate but it also prevents her from kissing him or taking off any more of their clothes.

"Can we just go to sleep? I can get home before my mom wakes up."

"Sure." Tara leans over and snaps off the light.

*

The morning sky is a flat gray. Soft light comes from all directions, dissolving even the thought of shadows. Shane takes one last look at Tara still asleep in bed and slides the window open. He could probably walk through the living room and out the front door, but for all he knows Tara's dad and his date are sprawled out on the ripped pleather couches. Or even worse, he could be awake and trying to be charming, teasing his date about how loud she got last night, about how his legend will carry on in the tales she tells. And he might be right. One night, Shane walked into the living room to find Glen and his beer-can dick passed out naked with a half-eaten burrito in his hand. Later, Evie overheard him and David laughing about it. She puckered her lips and said, *Don't matter what you got in your pants. Nasty is nasty.*

Shane drops down out of Tara's bedroom window. The cool morning air is sweet and green. He turns his face to the sun like a spring vine drinking in the day.

CHAPTER NINE

Shane flaked again. Or he chickened out. I don't know if anyone has a word for it when a guy avoids having sex with his girlfriend. I don't think I'm doing anything wrong. Other guys want me, all I have to do is walk down the street to know that. Sick. But I know Shane loves me. You can't fake caring about someone without the other person knowing it. I hope not anyways. And even if Shane might be faking it, the only reason guys play those games is to get girls to sleep with them. It doesn't make sense. The only reason he would have come over last night is to have sex, or because he loves me. Right? But if he loves me then he shouldn't have gotten all weird when I asked him about going to Toronto. Maybe he was planning to invite me and I wrecked the surprise by inviting myself. But I have a hard time believing that one. So maybe he loves me, but not enough to want me to go with him. He loves me, but not enough to have sex and get saddled with a kid. He loves me enough for right now but not enough for forever. Sounds like my mom.

Sometimes I open my eyes and I wonder if Mom is opening hers too. I feel her there like a mirror or an echo of myself. Like everything I do in the day, she's doing it at exactly the same time in exactly the same way. Just in a different place, in a different body. Older. Today is one of those days. I swing my legs out of bed and see her doing it too. I think of walking into the kitchen and she walks there with me, layered on top of me almost, like two universes stacked on top of each other. Doing everything in unison but unable to touch. I picture the two of us sitting cross-legged on my bed, face-to-face. I tell her all the things that I need to say, but when I do, her mouth opens at the same time. Problems spill out where there should be answers. Even in my dreams of her, she isn't enough.

> *Same shit different pile Dad says*
> *Talking about Mom*
> *and me*
> *See how that worked out*
> *Last we saw was the black*
> *Sweep of her ponytail*
> *Sun behind*
> *Dazzling the air*
> *Baby powder floating*
> *Fairy dust stopping time*
> *How can it be*
> *That the smell of home and*
> *the smell of lonely are the same?*

CHAPTER TEN

Uncle Pete's truck is parked at an angle, blocking off Shane's driveway. Marking his territory. Good thing Pete can't see when Shane takes a kick at the bumper; Pete'd lose it for sure. He used to be friends with some other guys around town, but whenever they got serious about a girl and stopped hanging out with him as much as he wanted, Pete would find some excuse to slash their tires or beat them up. After that, Pete would pick a new best friend and the whole thing would repeat itself. Jackie has tried setting him up with women over the years, but he's never showed much interest.

Shane closes the front door behind him, counting down the seconds until the inevitable run-in with his uncle. He kicks off his shoes and lines them up on the mat beside the others, keeping one eye on the broad hump of Pete's back straining against the wooden slats of a dining room chair.

Pete's voice booms from his seat, "So you don't come home at night now?" Shane uses the moment it takes to walk from the kitchen to the dining room to figure out how to respond. Jackie is sitting at the table with Pete, slowly ripping a paper napkin into downy shreds.

"I was at Kyle's," Shane lies. "Mom, you eat yet?"

Jackie doesn't look up. "Not yet."

Shane gives Pete a sour look. *Would it have killed him to make her some food?* Shane steps back into the kitchen and hunts for the cereal, shoving aside boxes of half-eaten crackers and slamming cupboard doors. His movements are jerky, more desperate than he wants to seem, but he can't help it. *Why is Pete even here!?* Maybe he needs money, or maybe Jackie asked him to come. Or he could be worried about his sister and decided to swing by … No. All of that is impossible. Whatever brought him here is bad. It's always something bad.

Shane swings a cupboard door shut with a bang. No cereal. He turns back toward the dining room and there she is. Destiny. She's standing there with the cereal box in her hand, just like she used to. He could swear she hid it on him sometimes, just to make him crazy. *Looking for this?* she would say with an impish little smirk.

There's no smile today though. Shane takes the box from her hand, then pulls a bowl out of the cupboard and pours the cereal inside. His heart slows down like it used to during a smudge. Like he has Destiny home again where she can be protected by their daily routine, where they're circled by an armor of small habits that over time become rituals. Prayers that keep them safe. Because Mom said that as long as they got their homework done and brushed their teeth and did the laundry, nothing bad could happen. Turns out lies don't become true even if everyone believes them.

When he sets the box down, Destiny is gone. The anger has gone too, leaving him hollowed out. Ready for battle.

Uncle Pete starts talking even before Shane makes it back into the dining room. "I just came from the store. Janice wants to get paid up front for the shit you guys ordered."

Shane sets the bowl of cereal down in front of Jackie. She mouths something, but if she actually spoke, it was too quiet to hear. "Just ask the band," he says. "The roof's halfway falling in already."

Uncle Pete shakes his head. "They're broke. They're always broke."

Shane wraps his arms around himself in a hug. "Well ..."

Pete holds out his hand to stop him. "It's gonna be fine, Shane. Your mom's got enough left over from when your dad died, so ..."

Shane does a quick mental calculation: his inheritance could cover either tuition or nearly all of the roof repairs, but no way it would cover both. And even if he uses it for university he'll still need to pay for housing, utilities, textbooks, food ...

"That money's for school," he snaps. "If I don't pay them this month I'm fucked."

"Maybe you should be thinking about taking care of your mom here instead of trying to run off."

Shane's vision goes streaky for a moment. "I'm not running anywhere. It's for school!"

Uncle Pete's chair scrapes against the plywood floor as he stands. He's a big guy and he's used to using his size to make sure he gets his way. Shane shrinks back a little. Uncle Pete notices and softens his voice. "You don't know how good you got it. You're smart. People like you. You could get a job on the council, do something at the mines ..."

Shane looks to Jackie for some kind of support, or even an

indication that she's aware of what is happening. Her eyes are empty. She's somewhere else entirely. The only sign that she's still with them is the pile of shredded napkin that she's slowly building in front of herself. *Why isn't she doing something? There's no way she would let Pete do this if she was normal.* After a lifetime of watching Jackie fiercely defend him and Destiny, it feels as though someone has stolen Jackie in the night. His real mother is somewhere else, screaming and tearing out her hair while he's left here with this pale husk. He's seen a Nish woman on TV talking about "stolen sisters." He knows she wasn't talking about this kind of theft, but still … no one can argue that his mother and sister are gone, and at least one of them is never coming back. The TV woman's words repeat over and over in his head like waves crashing on a shore: *stolen sisters stolen sisters stolen sisters stolen sisters stolen sisters …*

"Hey. I'm talking to you."

Shane closes his eyes and inhales deeply, wishing that a Drift would come for him in this moment.

Uncle Pete gestures to Jackie. "You better look around and figure out where your responsibilities are."

Shane snaps back to attention. "What about you? Maybe you should be taking care of your sister instead of putting it all on me."

Uncle Pete crosses his arms and looks away. "That's not my job. I'm just here 'cause Janice asked me."

Shane's eyes pass over Jackie and Uncle Pete. He tries to imagine what it means that the two of them lived a whole together life as brother and sister before Shane even came into the world. He wonders if there was a moment when their connection to each other broke, or if this chilly distance between them has always been there.

"All right, Pete, thanks for that. Message received. We don't need your help anyways. Get the fuck out of here."

Pete's eyes narrow into black slits. "Careful now."

Shane holds his eyes. "Or do you want to stay and cook lunch while I clean this place up?"

That does it. Uncle Pete grumbles and goes to the door. "Good luck finding the cash anywhere else." The door slams and the whole house shudders as though it's relieved he's gone.

Jackie rips the last bits of the napkin and lets them fall to the table. Her eyes drift up from the mysterious spot on the wall that's occupied her at least since Shane arrived, and maybe for some time before that. She's looking at Shane now. Her lips move like she wants to say something, but no sound comes out. Shane reaches forward to take the untouched cereal bowl from the table, just so he doesn't have to sit with her anymore. It makes him feel sick to be so close to her and so far away at the same time. In his mind the waves keep singing: *stolen sisters stolen sisters stolen sisters stolen sisters stolen sisters ...*

*

Shane doesn't have any idea where he's running to, but knows he has to leave the house or else burn it down. Right now. He races down the dirt road on foot, feeling like a bullet or maybe a heat-seeking missile, hurtling toward an unknown target. He imagines the world smearing suddenly into a flash of green and brown streaks like when they go into warp speed in *Star Trek*.

Birches, gravel, ragweed, and thistles all whip by in a blur of color. His feet drive into the ground one after the other. His blood pounds in time, his whole body made of rhythm. Energy pulses through him like the thrashing of a terrified snake. The only way out is to keep on running. So he does. He runs on and on, past the powwow grounds, past the store, the band office, and the youth center. His feet pick up speed until the air seems to shimmer and he rockets off the ground and into the sky.

He's on a Drift again, floating above the rez in a foggy bubble. He looks down and watches the movement below. The predictable flow of people picking up gas and buying smokes, the couple of families out on the water to check how high the rice has grown and maybe catch a fish or two. The secretaries at the band office pushing paper from one place to another, waiting for their next coffee break. Shane can see it all, and imagine their voices. He's heard them his whole life. When you're caught in the eddy of a place this small, you can't help thinking that every day will be the same as the one that came before it. You forget that life is moving forward whether you notice it or not. And then when something happens that's as final, as irreversible and messed up as Destiny's suicide ... you get burned. Burned alive, burned awake.

Shane's eyes snap open. He's on the ground, drenched with sweat. The inside of his mouth is almost painfully dry. He isn't sure where he is, but the comforting sound of water lapping against the shoreline sounds pretty close. He lifts his head off the ground and looks around. It's an old dirt track, with grass and wildflowers bristling between the ruts. Shane pulls himself up. The woods surrounding him could be anywhere on the lake. He listens to the water and the trees, looks at the line of the shore.

His gut, trained by a lifetime on this land, is telling him that he is somewhere on the other side of the lake, probably more than an hour's walk from home. But he's not going home. Not yet.

*

Ashley is standing outside the store with a poster for Girls' Day and a staple gun in her hands. She glances behind her disinterestedly when she hears Shane approach, then swivels back around to focus on her job. She staples the corners of the poster over layers of advertising for community events like the annual fishing derby, and homemade ads from people selling boats, snow machines, and wild rice. Ashley smiles at the solid *thunk* and *twang* that come when she pulls the trigger on the staple gun.

"Seen Janice?" Shane asks.

Ashley puts in another staple: *thunk-twang!* She answers without turning around. "In the office."

Shane nods his thanks and pushes past her to get inside the store. It's quiet today. It used to be that you could go in and get free coffee, but since Janice stopped doing that a few weeks ago, people have felt a lot less like going down to the store to chew the fat.

Shane breezes past the bags of chips and over to the door of Janice's office. Her mouth sets in a firm line when she sees Shane.

"I already talked to Pete. Your mom ordered all that stuff on credit. I've gotta send it back or sell it to someone else."

"You know what happened to my family, Janice. Mom's a mess. How am I supposed to get the money?"

Janice attempts a sympathetic smile, but it doesn't come across. "You're a smart kid, you'll figure it out."

"Come on, Janice. I know you make a shitload off this place. Just help us out for a little while. We'll get you the money eventually."

"Oooooh, eventually. Well that solves everything." Janice clasps her hands together. "Do you know what it costs just to have this stuff shipped up here? No? Of course you don't, because that's my job. You've got a month. That's all I can do."

Shane thinks: Can he do it in a month? He can pick up a bit of work here and there, but there's no job that's going to pay a kid seven grand for a month's work.

"It might as well be tomorrow," Shane says, then takes off before Janice can respond. On his way out, he pulls a bag of chips off the shelf and stuffs them into the pocket of his hoodie. Just let her try to stop him.

Shane ducks around to the back of the store, tearing into the bag of chips and trying to figure out what to do next. He sits on a pallet and looks up at the sky. The chewed-up chips form a paste that sticks to his teeth and the dry insides of his mouth.

The back door opens with the croak of a busted frog. Janice's eyebrows jump up so high they might have come off her head for a second when she sees Shane. "Geez! I didn't think anyone was back here."

"Didn't mean to scare you," Shane says. His tongue worms around in his mouth, picking bits of stolen chips from between his teeth. *Should have snagged a pop too, ha ha.*

Janice pulls a pack of smokes out of her purse and lights one up. She closes her eyes and takes a long, thirsty drag.

"What, did somebody stress you out or something?" Shane tries a smile.

Janice shakes her head and exhales a stream of smoke. "Just some stupid kid."

"Got an extra one of those?" Shane asks. He's never smoked anything in his life, so most people think he judges them for it.

Janice eyes him carefully, then slides a long, skinny cigarette out of the pack for him. Shane reaches for it and she snatches it away with a grin. "Don't tell your mom?"

Shane nods. "I definitely won't."

Janice slowly passes the cigarette to Shane. When the cigarette gets close, Shane reaches out and grabs it before she can change her mind.

"Thanks."

Janice touches the flame of her lighter to the tip of Shane's cigarette. He takes a few tentative puffs, trying not to choke.

"You been smoking long?" Janice is no dummy.

Shane pretends to be seriously interested in a group of kids playing in a grassy field of junk on the other side of the fence. "Yeah, a while."

Janice smiles and watches the kids with him. "Cute."

Shane glances nervously at Janice out of the corner of his eye. She seems like she's in a decent mood. He has nothing to lose. "So … You got any work I could do? Like, a job?"

Janice squints out at the messy yard full of junk where the kids are playing. "Yeah. Some odds and ends. Cleanup mostly."

"How much can you pay?"

Janice considers it. "Things are tough. No more than 80 bucks a day."

Shane takes a drag on the cigarette, frowning. It's not bad, but there's maybe a week or so of work for him to do back here. It's not near enough. Janice reads his face instantly.

"Take it or leave it."

Shane scans the debris-strewn yard. It's better than nothing. Not much, but still better.

*

The sun pushes down on Shane like one of those giant rollers that press hot asphalt on the highway. He wrestles the door off an old refrigerator and drags it over to a growing pile of garbage that Janice is going to have to truck to the dump. He's covered in sweat and grime, but it feels good to move his body. For the first time in weeks, his mind is clear. It's almost fun to set his muscles to work on a problem that already has a solution with definite edges and boundaries. Move the garbage so it can be hauled away. Toss a pallet in the Dumpster. Pull the nails out of this scrap wood. Stack and organize the inventory. Hard but simple.

"Whatcha doin'?"

Shane spins around to see Tara standing in the sun toying with a lollipop in her mouth.

"Uh ..." Shane can't tell her about the money. He shrugs. "Just doing some work."

Tara grins. "You can't help being good, can you? Helping your mom, helping Janice ..."

It's really not true, but Tara doesn't need to know.

"How about you take a break and come with me for a bit?"

Shane walks over to the bin with a piece of scrap wood and weighs his options. Home with mom. Working at a job that will keep him busy but never get him what he needs. Looking for David, who is probably still pissed at him, or ...

When he turns around, Tara flashes her sexiest smile at him. She's not going to take no for an answer. And maybe he doesn't want to say no anymore. Maybe Tara should be the one to come with him to Toronto. Maybe it's too hard, too painful to make a life here or anywhere with David. And maybe he and David would fall apart once they got to the loud, unfamiliar, hostile city. Maybe their heads are all messed up and once they fall in love— real love—with girls, their feelings for each other will seem small and silly. Like kids playing a game, practicing for the real world. People say that happens. They say some guys have a thing with a friend when they're teenagers and eventually grow out of it. Who knows? Maybe going to Toronto with Tara will be like planting a seed; first he'll commit to a life with her and then love will grow from there. That makes sense. It has to make sense. He and Tara can make it work if they want it badly enough. And they do, he's pretty sure of it.

He'll focus on school for the first bunch of years and then get a job with the city as an engineer or a planner. And Tara will … Shane has no idea what Tara would want to do. Wait tables? Model? If there's something she wants, she's never mentioned it. Or maybe he wasn't listening. Should he have asked? Shane looks up at the birds flying overhead and pushes the cluttered mess of thoughts away. He can ask what she wants anytime. The only thing that matters is that she loves him. And he cares about her too—it's not all fake. Maybe they can make it work. Of course they can. It could be worse.

*

The empty lot is a crowded dreamscape of waving yellow and purple blooms. Tara jumps over an old tricycle as she dashes through the ragweed and thistle. Shane dodges around rocks, trying to catch up. The strap of his backpack swings and spins in his slippery hands. Their sneakers crash through the grass like the thunder of November waves on Lake Superior.

"I'm gonna get you!" Shane yells.

Tara shoves hard against the door. It scrapes noisily against the unfinished floor, but it doesn't move much. She tries again. This time the door swings open and she tumbles inside. Shane tosses his groceries down and skitters behind her. The house is empty, long-since abandoned. The floors have been stripped down to chipboard and the drywall is gone. Skeletal joists outline where the rooms would have been, looking like a rib cage closing around Tara as she runs to the back. Generations of teenagers have dragged in old couches and pinned up floral sheets to give the illusion of privacy. Tara flops down on a mattress in the corner of what once must have been a bedroom. Within moments, Shane is on top of her.

"Ha! I got you."

"And now what are you going to do with me?"

This is it. This is what every guy wants. Or at least it should be. Tara could have anyone at school and she chose him.

"Maybe I'll ... take you to Toronto with me."

Tara opens her mouth to speak, but nothing comes out.

"Still want to go?" Shane asks.

Tara lights up like a little kid. "Of course! Don't be stupid!"

Shane's smile starts to feel forced. *What am I doing?* But if he's made a mistake it's too late to turn back now.

"Someone's gotta take care of you," Tara says. "Little Nish in the big city."

It wasn't that long ago that Jackie was the one taking care of him, but when he tries to remember, all of it feels like a movie he watched once, or a story he heard about someone else.

Shane nuzzles into Tara's neck and kisses the soft skin below her ear. He thinks about what will happen next, planning their session like a recipe. There will need to be a certain amount of kissing, a certain amount of playing with her breasts. He'll have to rub against her like he wants to have sex but he's holding back. Usually he can get away with doing it for a little under an hour before …

Tara has skipped ahead. She is tugging at his belt and opening his fly so that he can get his jeans off. Unsure what else to do, he goes along with it. He can only get them just past his knees with Tara straddling him, so she grabs the cuffs and yanks them the rest of the way off. Her giggle sounds like a music box.

Tara runs her hand over his crotch and pulls at the waistband of his underwear. Shit, he isn't hard. That's embarrassing. Shane looks up at the widow. "I wish we could make it dark in here." Without the distraction of seeing her, they would just be bodies.

"I like being able to see your eyes." Tara's face twitches like she's about to sneeze. Shane doesn't have long to wonder why. "I love you," Tara says.

Shane's brain stops. This is the first time either of them has said it. It should feel good, better than good, but all he can think of is the back tires of Uncle Pete's tires spinning in the snow when he got stuck in the ditch last winter.

"I love you, Shane." When she says it the second time, it sounds like an accusation. She holds his eyes, waiting. It's not hot in here but Shane's hands are gummy with sweat.

"I ... love you too." Shane steals a quick look to see Tara's reaction. He didn't think it sounded believable, but she doesn't seem to notice or care. In a moment she is on him again, her tongue fighting inside his mouth. Shane has never been to the ocean but this must be what the undertow feels like: an unstoppable, invisible force dragging him down to someplace dark and alien where he can't breathe. Tara comes up for air.

"Are we doing this?" Shane asks.

"Do you want to?"

"Yeah. I guess. I think so." He tells himself that if she wants him this much, maybe this is where he needs to be. Maybe he can love her too. It could be worse.

Tara smiles at him. It's happening. They're going to do it. The moment hangs in the air and stretches out time. It feels so long that Shane wonders if this might not be happening after all. Like maybe time will start to run backward and he and Tara will never have sex, and Destiny's corpse will recompose until she is full of life and back to sleeping in the bedroom down the hall from him again. But no. That doesn't really happen. His physics teacher said that time isn't necessarily linear, but for Shane, time stubbornly refuses to turn backward. It keeps putting one hairy foot down in front of the other, no matter how badly he wants it to stand still or turn around or do anything other than go forward.

Tara leans over to her bag and rummages around for a condom. "I know it's in here ... I got it from Berta's last week." After a moment, she pops back up. "Do you know how to put it on?"

"Yeah." He rips open the shiny foil square and pulls the slimy latex out of its package. He's only ever played with one once before. When he opened it up he thought there was something wrong with it because it smelled so gross. But this one has the same medicinal stink, so it must be normal. Shane pinches the tip and slides it on. He tries to think if there is anything else he is supposed to do. It should be pretty straightforward from here. There was something about gripping it from the base to slide it off after …

Shane kneels over Tara. "Are you ready?"

Tara nods. "Just go slow, okay?"

Shane pulls her legs apart. The heat of her body pulls him closer. The smell is sweet and sour, familiar and totally unlike anything he's ever imagined. People used to call them *private parts*. And it feels like that—*private*. Like she's sharing a secret he knows he'll never keep.

"Is everything okay?" Tara asks.

Shane wonders how long he spaced out for. "Yeah."

Okay. So this is really happening. Shane takes a deep breath and tries to push himself inside her. Tara's face twists uncomfortably and she pushes him away.

"Can I do it?" Shane lifts his hands away and allows her to guide him. Tara looks at him with perfect trust. He feels sick. She adjusts her hips and tugs at him like a warm current. Unbelievably warm. It's too much. He's dragged under. Pinpricks dance over his arms and legs and before he realizes it, he's falling into a Drift. It sucks him farther into the darkness of the salt and weeds than he ever imagined he would go. He knows he should panic; there's danger in deep water. He could die down here at any moment. The pressure could collapse his lungs. But it doesn't. The trick of staying alive underwater is that you can't breathe it in.

The raspy sound of the front door opening yanks him out of the Drift. Tara's eyes are wide. Footsteps in the hall.

"Shit." The steps get louder. Tara searches for her underwear.

"Who's there?" Shane asks. David's head emerges from around the corner, just as Tara jumps under the covers. Shane is hanging out all over the place. The look on David's face is horrible. Just … pure pain.

"Get the fuck out, you pervert!" Tara yells.

David rushes back down the hall and out of the house, leaving Tara and Shane alone. Tara looks down at herself and says, "I think he got an eyeful." Shane stays quiet, grateful to have the brief task of finding his clothes.

Tara flops back down on the bed. "Whatever. I heard he's gay anyways."

CHAPTER ELEVEN

I can't believe we did it. Me and Shane were just messing around in the abandoned house by the end of the main road when out of nowhere Shane asked me to come to Toronto. I said yes (of course) and then we started messing around. He was being awkward about it, as usual. I don't know why but right then I realized that nothing will ever be mine unless I go after it. And that includes Shane. So I reached down and took his pants off and climbed on top of him. There was a clumsy bit while we got the condom on and then he was inside me. Just like that. I feel stupid after all of that worrying and wondering about whether or not he wanted to be with me. Turns out he just needed me to take charge. Someone should have warned me it would hurt so bad, though. I was actually kind of glad when David interrupted us. We had just started, but I was ready for it to be over. Hopefully it'll get better the more we do it.

It felt good to make something happen, even if it's just sex.

Is that how the world works? You just stand up and go for what you want and then you get it? I always feel like I need to ask permission. My dad used give me a spank if I did anything without asking, but now that I'm older maybe I don't have to ask anymore. For the longest time all I wanted was to be left alone, and if I was quiet and nice then people would more or less do that. To the point where I think people forgot about me sometimes. But what if being left alone isn't enough? This thing with Shane has me thinking that it might not be crazy to want to write. Maybe getting people to listen to me is as simple as announcing that I have something to say and demanding that they listen. It's something to try, anyways.

I don't know what I want from you.
Just your body brain heart
spirit skin memory
mouth future dreams
that's all.
I want it all.

Swallow me up
Toss me
like a pebble caught in the curl
of a wave.
I want to feel the force of you
wet and rushing
Inside and out

I'm not asking. I'm telling.
Swallow me up!
Carry me on your crest
Smooth my rough edges.
Show me as I am
Hard and glistening.

CHAPTER TWELVE

Shane's been working out behind the store for a few hours, but he can't seem to stop himself from checking his phone every ten minutes to see if there is something new from David. So far, nothing since last night around midnight. Shane keeps his head down and keeps working. He'll check again once he clears the rest of this half-buried hose.

"What are you doing?"

Shane's head snaps up. David is standing by the propane shed.

"I'm working. What's it look like?" It comes out sharper than he means it to.

"What for? I thought you had insurance money from your dad."

Shane shoves the blade of his shovel into the dirt and pries it back. There's no point in explaining anything. It's not like David can fix it.

"You going to the talking circle tomorrow?" David asks.

Roberta has been holding circles for Destiny just about every week since she died. Shane yanks at the nest of old hose until it begins to slide out of the muck.

"It might feel good to talk about her," David says.

"Yeah I guess …" Shane drops the hose and wipes his hands on his rough cotton work pants. David takes a step closer to him. He can be relentless. "I guess I could tell everyone how I was with my boyfriend all night when I should have been watching my sister."

David freezes. It's a low blow and Shane knows it, but there's no going back now. He picks up the pile of muddy hose and drags it to the Dumpster. Even with his back turned, he can feel David shrinking away inside, drying up. But if he's going away with Tara then he should get the hard stuff with David finished, no matter how much it hurts. No matter how much every instinct in his body is telling him not to push David away. He had told Tara *I love you* just last night. That counts for something. Right or wrong, a choice has to be made. Shane's mind flashes David's wounded face when he saw Tara and Shane in bed together. David is better off without him.

Shane tosses the mess in the Dumpster and walks back to David. "I don't know why you're even here," Shane says. "You saw me with Tara. She's coming with me to Toronto."

"But I thought …"

"You thought what? You thought I would just wait around forever?"

David stands still, clenching and unclenching his fists. Shane scans the yard, looking for his next task. If he focuses on David any longer, he'll break. He avoids David's eyes, but he can feel them on his face like blind, fumbling fingers. Reading him. Trying to understand.

Shane turns at the sound of a heel on gravel. David is striding past the pumps and away from Shane.

Shane calls out, "That's it? You're just gonna let me go with her!?"

David's shoulders are hunched. If he heard Shane, he doesn't show it.

Shane tips his water bottle back for a drink. The sun-warmed water trickles down his throat as he surveys the back lot. There's still a shit-ton of work to be done. Shane sets his water down, and a stack of old sheet metal catches his eye. He thumbs through the pile. It isn't clear whether it's meant to be scrap or inventory, but as Uncle Pete once told him: *Sometimes it's easier to beg forgiveness than ask permission.*

*

Shane has to stop to adjust the metal sheets in his hands. They're heavier than they looked back at Janice's and those sharp edges wasted no time cutting into his fingers. When Shane crosses over the hill, he sees Evie walking up the steps to his house. He nearly calls out to her, until he remembers the stolen sheet metal he's carrying. He walks down the hill sticking close to the tree line. He hides behind some shrubs near the door to avoid having to explain himself to Evie.

"Hellooo … Jackie?!" Evie calls. "I know you're home—I can hear the TV!" Evie tries the doorknob, but it's locked. "What're you locking the door for? You got nothing to steal!" Evie chuckles to herself.

The sound of the TV stops. Shane hears the telltale hissing of Jackie's slippers dragging across the linoleum and then the door opens. He can't see his mother's face from his hiding place, but he can see a bit of Evie through the leaves. The thin lines at the corners of her mouth tap out a signal that would read as clear as a billboard to anyone who grew up with a certain kind of auntie. Before she even opens her mouth to speak, her face is saying: *I love you, but you better get ready and listen to your auntie now, cuz I know a couple a things about a couple a things!*

"Aanii," Evie says, greeting her in Anishinaabemowin.

Jackie is quiet.

Evie clears her throat and pulls a box of hair dye out of a plastic shopping bag. "You probably have half left over from last time, but I picked up some more just in case."

Silence again. Evie's eyes move over the map of Jackie's face, looking for a way in.

"You didn't need to do that," Jackie says at last.

Evie gives her a wide winking smile. She's playing it sweet today. "Aah—good to be busy," she says. "Keeps me young, even if I don't look it."

Shane sees Jackie's hand curl around the edge of the doorjamb. "I'm not feeling that good today."

"Want me to make some tea?"

"I think I'm gonna head back to bed."

Shane holds his breath to see what Evie will do next. Sometimes being the nice auntie doesn't work as well as she'd like.

"It's not good for you to be in there with her things all the time," Evie says. Shane wishes he could see his mother's face.

"I'm fine." Jackie's hand slips out of sight, and the door creaks like it's beginning to close.

"You gonna do the giveaway next May?"

Jackie pauses in the doorway. The question hangs there like a hummingbird. Shane has wondered it himself, but he hasn't dared to ask. On the first anniversary of a death, people often hold a gathering to give away the things that belonged to the one who passed. Everyone takes a little something—a fishing rod, a knife, a favorite mug—allowing the whole community to share in their memory.

Jackie pulls the door back open. Shane imagines her standing defiant, a glimmer of who she used to be.

"I'm not going to do that."

Evie's eyebrows lift above the rim of her glasses. "But you have to do something for her."

"Don't look at me like that," Jackie snaps. "I'm sick of you coming over here all the time, pretending you care about us so you don't feel guilty."

Evie slowly puts the box of hair dye back in the shopping bag. Sadness settles through her joints and ropy muscles; it nestles in her shoulders and curls up in the folds of her neck. "When you need something, you know where I live."

After a moment, the door closes with a hollow click. Evie shifts her weight and walks slowly from the house like a pack horse with a heavy load. Before she leaves, Evie casts a look into the bushes where Shane is hiding. Her eyes are terrible—there's no way she can see him in there, but there are other ways of knowing.

CHAPTER THIRTEEN

There isn't much light left, but it's good enough to work by. The muddy summer dusk likes to linger. Birds flit home to their nests, crisscrossing the sky with groggy bats whose night of hunting has just begun. Shane props the metal ladder against the side of his house. The sheet metal is too heavy and awkward to carry with one hand, so he has to hold it in front of him while he climbs the ladder hands-free.

Once on top of the roof, Shane takes his toolbox and the sheet metal over to a place where the shingles are curling up and the wood underneath is showing through. As he gets closer, the roof starts to feel like an old sponge. He prays it will hold his weight. The last thing he needs right now is to fall through and break his neck. He puts the sheet metal down over what looks like the worst part of the roof. There's probably more to fixing a leak than this, but even a crappy patch job will be better than nothing.

He sorts through a box of nails, uncertain even how long they should be. He chooses one that seems medium size, and holds it to a corner of the sheet metal. He taps down with his hammer, but it bounces back. Not enough force. Shane adjusts his grip on the handle and tries again with confidence, like someone who knows what they're doing. The nail punches through the metal with a satisfying *thunk* and then a clatter when the hammer connects with the metal. He gets up on his knees and looks around to see if the noise has attracted the attention of the neighbors. All is quiet. Shane bends down again, picks up another nail, and hammers it through the metal and into the tarry shingles. Once he has all four corners nailed down, Shane admires his handiwork. It's not going to earn any prizes for prettiest roof on the rez, but hopefully it'll keep the damage from spreading any more than it already has.

Shane's cell phone vibrates with a text from Tara. Her name pulses like a threat. Something about her scares him. Shane shoves the phone in his pocket and but keeps his hand wrapped tightly around it. Maybe he's not allowed to brush her off anymore, now that they had sex. But it might not matter—it's not like it was twenty years ago. Back in the day, messing around with David wouldn't have even been an option. Shane pictures Tara and David tied back-to-back in a wooden canoe. He grasps the bow of the boat in both hands and shoves it hard, sending them out over the glassy lake. They remain silent and still, their eyes locked on him as they fade into the air and wind and water, conveniently erased.

Shane lets out a deep breath he didn't realize he was holding. The world feels grayer, less open to dreaming than it did a few minutes before. *The real world.* His metal tools glow eerily with the last traces of light. Shane gets down on his knees to finish his work. He swings the hammer again and again, focusing on the placement of the nails and the tensing of his muscles, allowing himself to disappear at last into the job at hand.

*

When he gets back inside, Jackie is nowhere to be found and the door to Destiny's room is closed. This is the new normal. He can't recall the last time he saw her anywhere other than in that bed, or on her way to the bathroom, or maybe shuffling to the fridge. At least this way he mostly doesn't have to see what's become of his mom. He can ignore how completely she has been obliterated, her spirit put out like a candle by his sister's murder. *Murder.* He would never say it out loud but it's true. His sister was brutally murdered, but he can't even be pissed off about it or hunt for revenge because she was both the victim and the murderer. *Murder. Self-murder. Murderer.* It would have been easier if someone else killed her. He would have someone to hate without the rest of his shitty feelings getting in the way.

Shane looks down at the box of spaghetti in his hand. *Heat water to a rolling boil, then submerge.* Bubbles of air form in the bottom of the pot and rise to the surface of the water. *Is that what a rolling boil looks like? Good enough.* He tosses half into the pot and leaves the box on the stovetop.

His phone buzzes. This time it's Kyle: *Auntie wants to see you. Start dealing and I'll twist yr dick off.* Shane starts to type a message telling Kyle there's no way he's ever dealing for Debbie or anybody else, but then he deletes it. Better to leave all doors open, even if you're pretty sure they lead to hell. It's not going to kill him to have options. Shane types *K* and hits send.

Jackie wanders into the kitchen, rubbing her eyes. "Sounded like there was somebody on the roof."

Shane eyes the pot of pasta. A few spiky ends slowly droop

over the edge like a pair of spindly legs over the lip of a bathtub. Jackie stands in the middle of the kitchen looking like she can't remember where she is or why she came in there in the first place.

"You take your pills, Mom?" Shane passes the amber plastic bottle to her. Jackie takes it, but she doesn't make a move to do anything about it. Before Destiny died, Jackie prayed every day. She said the smell of sage settled her nerves and focused her thoughts on living her life in a good way. She told him that she could feel the spirit moving through everything, from her own body to the deer in the bush and the grandfather rocks beneath her feet. She always put down tobacco when she entered someone else's territory; she always came with a song when she was asked to feast someone's spirit name, and brought food for the fire keepers at a sweat. But after Destiny, she had told Evie that nothing had spirit anymore. The rocks were just rocks. Their bodies were only meat. Even the medicines were empty, a handful of dried herbs. It hurt him to see her like that. He wished she would pray, or at least try.

Shane pushes stray ends of pasta deeper into the pot. "Supper'll be about twenty minutes," he says. Jackie glides to the sink like she's being pulled along by an alien tracking beam. Next thing he knows she'll be floating out the window on her way to the mother ship. *Ha ha, mom—mother ship.*

"I think Evie dropped off your hair dye. It's on the table there." Jackie doesn't seem to hear him. "Why didn't Evie do your hair for you?" His mom isn't listening. Her arm drifts away from her body with a slow, deliberate movement, like a sleep-walking dancer.

The squeal of the smoke alarm cuts through the air. A piece of pasta has fallen on the burner and set the edge of the box on fire. Shane swats at the flames until the box stops burning, then hustles over to fan smoke away from the squealing alarm. Jackie's hands are clasped tightly over her ears and her face is scrunched up like she's getting ready for someone to hit her. The sound cuts out. Shane goes to his mother and gently pulls her hands away from her ears.

"It's okay, Mom. It stopped."

Without saying a word, Jackie floats back to Destiny's room. She pauses in the doorway. "Help me dye my hair later?"

Shane doesn't know whether this is a sign of her beginning to bounce back, or further evidence of her retreat. "Of course," he says. "I'll bring you some food first." Jackie steps into the dark bedroom and closes the door softly behind her. Shane looks back at the pot, still bubbling away on the stove. The pasta is going to be mushy, but it's better than nothing.

*

Jackie sits in a kitchen chair with her head hanging back into the sink. With the layer of thick black dye, it looks like she's wearing a toque made of axle grease. Shane stands over her and carefully peels a layer of plastic wrap from her scalp. It's clammy, like the wrapping on a marked-down package of chicken legs. He reaches out with his pinkie—the only clean finger—to turn on the tap. The water gurgles down the drain with a deep, sucking voice. Shane fills a little teacup under the stream of warm water, then passes it over Jackie's head like a priest administering some kind of rites. If ever there was a time for an invocation, this was it. *But what kind?* Jackie looks at him expectantly. Shane splashes water down along Jackie's hairline, resisting the urge to pray.

"Is that too hot?"

"No, it's nice."

Shane runs his fingers through Jackie's sticky hair, relishing the feeling of the warm, slippery dye between his fingers. He massages her scalp and his fingers turn black. It feels as though he is pulling something evil out of his mother's body and drawing it in through his own skin. He has to fight the impulse to turn the taps on full blast and scrub his hands raw. Because that would be crazy—it's just hair dye. Only dollars at the store in Kenora. No dark magic there.

"You should call Evie."

Jackie closes her eyes.

"Did you hear me?" Shane asks.

"Mmmmmm …" Jackie says. Her body is in the room but she's somewhere far away. "Make sure you get the back, okay? Evie misses it sometimes."

Shane reaches around to massage and rinse the dye from the back of Jackie's head. She pushes the weight of her head back against his fingers, almost but not quite smiling.

"The other day I found a card you made for Destiny when you were little." Jackie's voice is creaky. "There was a drawing of you with boxing gloves on, and you promised you would beat up anybody that gave her trouble. Unless it was Chuck Liddell or The Rock." Shane looks away, hoping she doesn't notice the tremble in his fingers. He should be able to enjoy this mood of hers, but knowing that it won't last wrecks it. Her smile cuts into

Shane like a blade. He imagines her asking, *Does that hurt? Tell me where it hurts, baby. Tell Mommy where it hurts.*

He feels Destiny in the room before he notices a second pair of hands massaging the dye out of Jackie's hair. He takes in every detail: the chipped nails and the pale scar that curls over the caramel skin of her middle finger. Missing her is more than painful; it's disorienting, like losing one of his senses. He tries not to blink, hoping somehow it'll keep her here. It feels so good to have her beside him, but each time she leaves, it's like he's been torn open and stitched back together again. Better but also worse. Full of happiness when he sees her, but terrified of the pain that will come when she leaves. Destiny pushes closer to him than she would have in life, but there's no warmth there, no weight from her body telling him it's real. Not even when her fingers brush against his in the tangle of their mother's hair. Shane turns to look at his sister's face, but she's gone again. She never stays. The loneliness comes rushing in, dark and suffocating.

"Did you ever do that for her?"

Shane struggles to pick up the thread of their conversation. "Do what?"

"Fight," Jackie says. "Defend her like you said in your card."

His mother hasn't said this many words to him in weeks and of course one of the first things she says turns out to be an accusation.

"She looked tough with her piercings and that but she wasn't," Jackie says, almost in a whisper. "My girl was gentle …" Her face relaxes. The light in her eyes recedes like taillights in the distance.

Shane takes a deep breath to steady himself. "Okay, I think we're almost done. Want me to get the mirror?"

"Nah. You're so good. How did you get to be so good, eh?"

Shane carefully rinses the dye from the hair around Jackie's face. He rubs his thumb against a black smudge on her temple, careful not to get water in her eyes. The smudge on her skin lightens some, but she'll be stuck with it awhile. Shane looks down at the blue-black stain on his open palms. *Marked forever,* he thinks. But then he remembers, *Nothing lasts forever.*

*

Shane doesn't know where he wants to go, but his feet are carrying him to the water. It should be quiet now, unless some kids have decided to build a fire. Most of them would rather be someplace inside though. He unzips his hoodie and lets the cool fingers of the breeze run over his neck. So much has felt unreal in the past few weeks, the chill reminds him that he is still here.

An inky shape is moving down by the water. Shane stops and crouches in the shadow of some rocks. He hadn't planned on running into anyone. Whether or not he makes his presence known depends on who is there. After a moment of watching, Shane recognizes the stiff posture, the nervous hands. It's David.

David stops what he's doing and looks around, an animal scanning for danger. "Shane?"

Shane shrinks closer to the ground. David squints into the thick shadows along the unlit beach. Black water spreads out in front of him. Curling mist from the lake is the only clue that David isn't hovering in the endless darkness of space. David stands there looking for a full minute before he squats down again and pulls out a knife. He takes a plastic pop bottle into his hands and cuts into it with the point of his knife, slicing through the sides to remove the base. He fumbles through his pockets, then nestles a piece of paper inside the bottom. A lighter sparks, and something catches. *The wick from a candle?* A pale yellow flame illuminates a photo of Destiny tucked inside the cutoff bottle. Shane isn't close enough to make out the details, but he doesn't need to. It's her school photo, the one they used at her funeral and memorial. He's searched that picture for clues a thousand times.

David sets the little shrine on the surface of the lake. It weaves and lists with the movement of the water, but it stays afloat. Shane wants to get up, but his body won't let him. His feet are heavy and his fingertips prickle like at the beginning of a Drift. Blood pounds in his head. David gives the makeshift shrine a gentle nudge to carry it out into the darkness of the lake. It slowly turns as it floats away, hiding and then revealing Destiny's face. David breaks a cigarette open and sprinkles dry flakes of tobacco over the water while he whispers a prayer in Anishinaabemowin.

David stands up and tilts his head to the sky. He arches his back in a stretch, then straightens again, letting his gaze settle on the spot where Shane is hiding. It's impossible that David can see him—Shane can't even see his own hands—but it can't be a coincidence either. Shane doesn't move. David turns back to watch the shrine on the water. After a minute or so, David turns back to the dark place where Shane is holding his breath, as if to offer him a final opportunity to show himself. When Shane stays where he is, David shakes his head and walks away. Destiny's shrine winks from the water like a fallen star.

Shane steps out of the shadows. His body aches with cold. He picks his way over the rocks and toward the lights of the powwow grounds. When he looks back at the lake for the light from Destiny's shrine, there is nothing there.

*

Back at home, Shane puts away the last couple of plates from the drying rack, then sits at the kitchen table in front of his laptop. Jackie has gone into hibernation for the night. He wonders what she'll do when he isn't there. He'll probably get a call from Evie after a month in Toronto, saying that his mom was found mummified in Destiny's bedroom, dried out like a piece of jerky.

Not funny.

Thoughts like that give him the feeling that his brain is actually working to destroy him. Shane finds a few new messages in his email—notifications from Facebook and junk from Roberta, but one stands out from the rest. The subject line reads: *Student Housing.* Shane clicks on it, and a photograph appears. Happy multiethnic students walk through a green campus framed by stately stone buildings. The glow of their promising futures is spread over their faces like icing. *We're rich! We're lucky! We can do any goddamn thing we want to! Are you sure you got into this university!?*

Shane presses a button that says: *Click Here to Register for Campus Housing,* and then enters in a series of numbers and letters when the site asks him for his student ID. A message pops up: *Our system indicates that you have not yet paid your enrollment confirmation deposit. Please pay this amount in order to register for student housing.* Shane looks back at the photo of smiling students from his email. *You seem poor! Do they let poor kids go here?* Shane closes the laptop and shoves it to the other side of the table.

CHAPTER FOURTEEN

I made the mistake of telling Ashley that Shane and I had sex for the first time. I thought she would laugh, but she got really quiet and then ripped into me because she said I had been lying to her this whole time. Which I guess I was. I never thought of it as lying, but she was really hurt. She said that the only reason she had sex with Kyle was because Shane and I looked so happy. She thought having sex would make them happy too. I wanted to laugh at that one, but I knew better. Ashley seems tough and she makes fun of me so much that it was hard to take her feelings seriously. I never thought she liked me enough that I would be able to hurt her, you know?

It seemed like she started to feel better when I told her Shane has ignored me since we had sex. That's the way it goes, *she said. I wish I had nodded my head and left it at that, but I had to go and read her the poem that I wrote about having sex the first time. She snatched the notebook out of my hands and ran around my room yelling out,* Swallow me up! I want to be perfect! *It made me want to die. When you're a kid people tell you that if you go out in the world and show people who you really are, nothing can touch you. I call bullshit on that. If I had a kid I would tell her that most everyone in this world wants something from you. I would tell her to lock up everything that is good and real and only offer it to the ones who earn it. I would teach her to be impenetrable. A mountain of a woman with a heart of lava.*

If You Were My Baby ...

If you were my baby and I were your mother
I would rub you with sandpaper
Till you hardened to rock.

If you were my baby and I were your mother
I'd feed you fresh chilies
Until you breathed flames.

If you were my baby and I were your mother
I would hide you from men
Even your father.

If you were my baby and I were your mother
I would feed you whole cities
Until none were left.

If you were my baby and I were your mother
I would never be happy
And neither would you.

CHAPTER FIFTEEN

Shane feels the big drum vibrating even before his ears pick out the sound in the distance. As he gets closer, the pounding rhythm and the melody rise out of the shrieks of birds and the lapping of the lake. Tara is already at the community center, watching the men's drum group practice. She stubs out her cigarette when Shane arrives.

"You don't have to do that. I know you smoke."

Tara shrugs. "I know."

Shane knows he should say more—he should apologize for being out of touch and ask her how she is—but David is sitting so close, drumming with the circle of men, and he can't stop looking at him.

Tara feels for Shane's hand. "When do you want to talk about Toronto?"

"Anytime, I guess." Talking to Tara while watching David is like having to sit in class in the middle of June when all he wants to do is run out into the sun.

David's eyes drift over Shane without a flicker of recognition.

Any hope Shane has for an easy reunion with David blows away like smoke.

"I think we should get an apartment way up high," Tara says, "so we can see the whole city." She slides her hand into his back pocket.

Shane nods, barely listening, his heart beating in time with the drum, willing David to look at him again, to give Shane a sign that he'll forgive him.

"I'll probably have to get a job down there too. Maybe wait-ressing or something?"

"Yeah, that'd be good. You're pretty good with people."

The drum keeps on. Shane's *niinag* thickens, twitching to life with the drum. Some songs are like a heartbeat that fills up the dark, empty places inside you with light, but today this song feels like … sex. He hopes it's not disrespectful for a powwow song to get him going like this. Shane shifts his weight to the other foot, using the opportunity to tuck himself into the waist-band of his jeans.

David's eyes connect with Shane's and that's it. He's a goner. It's one of the biggest mysteries of life that they can look at each other with a bunch of people around and no one sees or senses the fire between them. It feels like everyone for miles around should be blinded. Like the heat coming off the two of them should singe their hair and melt their faces. That's not normal, right? Most couples don't feel like that. *I have to get him back.* This is too good to walk away from without a fight.

The drummers come to the end of their song, but the inside of Shane's body is still shaking. David glances over his shoulder at Shane before helping the drummers carry the chairs and the drum inside. *Was his look supposed to say, "Follow me" or "Fuck off"?*

"Holaaaaah! Where the party at?" Kyle and Ashley walk up the road toward Shane and Tara.

Shane glances to the door of the center, where David has disappeared with the other drummers. The drum is still beating in his blood. "I'll see you guys in a bit, okay?" Shane gives Tara a peck on the cheek and jogs lazily toward the community center.

"See you at the circle?" Tara calls out.

*

Shane's shoes squeak on the freshly waxed floor of the community center. The halls are lit with the same tired fluorescents that flicker in the school. David stands alone in front of the door to the boiler room. Shane slows his walk, scanning David to predict what's likely to happen next. David opens the door to the boiler room and slips inside. *Is this "Come in here so I can give you shit in private" or ... ?*

The room is lit by the glowing red exit sign above the door. David is at the other end of the room, a fuzzy shape standing in the shadows. Shane locks the door but he doesn't move. Usually David would have said something by now. Shane takes a step deeper inside the room. The outline of David's body becomes clear, like in the moments after a Drift when the melting mass of shapes and colors crystallize back into the real world: His house with its scent of wet wood and onion skins. His bed with the scratchy blankets and maps of all the places he wants to go. And here in front of him, David, who he loves beyond the point of fear.

David, who carries him to a place that is more alive and humbling and dangerous than anything he has ever known.

Shane takes another step forward and reaches out for David. His heartbeat throbs under his cotton T-shirt.

"I'm so sorry," Shane says.

"Shhh. I know." Voices echo from the hallway. "You sure the door's locked?" David asks.

Shane nods and leans in to kiss David. David opens his mouth and pulls Shane deeper. His mouth is full of slippery heat, sharp teeth, and a sweet-sour taste that he can never get enough of. Shane grabs a fistful of David's hair and pushes him against the wall. They pull at each other's clothes until they're bare. Shane circles his arms around David's chest, savoring the feel of skin on skin, of their eager *niinagan* pressed together. Shane closes his eyes and lets go. This is the only thing better than a Drift. It's the same weightlessness, the same feeling of being completely unmoored, but instead of floating disconnected above his body, he is free inside it. Energy explodes within him, electrifying his lips, his skin, his tongue, fusing his whole body and spirit together the way they were meant to be.

Afterward, their tangled bodies cool on the grit of the concrete floor. Shane takes a slow inventory of his body, recognizing each part as separate from David's. *My arm. David's shoulder. My back. David's hand. My scalp. David's wrist. My stomach. David's chest. My toes. David's hips …*

David points at a footprint on the ceiling. "How do you think that got there?"

"Prolly some kind of crazy sex moves." Shane starts to laugh, but stops when he hears it ricochet back at him from the ceiling.

David strokes Shane's chest. "So are you gonna tell me what's going on with school?"

Shane shrugs. "I might be kinda screwed. I don't know—Roberta told me I'm not even registered on this rez." David waits for more. "Hopefully I'll figure something out. There's got to be options."

"And if you can't figure it out, you stay here?"

"You wish." Shane smiles.

"I do."

Shane doesn't want to have this talk. He grabs his phone out of his jeans. It's two o'clock. "Shit. We've got to go. The circle is starting."

*

Shane looks through the glass panel in the door. Fifteen or so teenagers are scattered around a circle of blue folding chairs while Roberta moves from person to person with the smudge bowl. Shane glances behind him. The hallway is empty, no sign of David. He's probably still in the bathroom trying to rinse the imaginary smell of sex off his skin. Shane slips inside and scans the circle until he finds a seat next to Tara.

Tara whispers, "I saved it for you," and smiles.

Roberta fans the smudge. Thick smoke curls around Lyndahl's head. He's one of Ashley's cousins, but he mostly hangs out with the gamers. Lyndahl says, *Miigwech*," and steps away. Ashley is next. She can barely be bothered to go through the motions, which is pretty standard for her. As though waving her floppy wrists through the smoke is doing the rest of us a huge favor. When she's done, Ashley steps away and says, *"Miigwech,"* under her breath, like she's throwing something embarrassing in the garbage.

When it's Shane's turn, he closes his eyes and breathes deeply, filling his lungs with the spicy medicine. It's like clear skies, happy tears, wet leaves, and fresh kindling. If goodness had a smell this would be it. Shane waves the smoke around his feet and legs: *so that I will walk in a good way.* He presses it to his eyes: *so that I will see in a good way,* and to his mouth: *so that I will speak good words.* He washes his hands in the smoke: *to help me do good work,* and brushes it over his arms: *so that I will love and support the people around me.*

Shane opens his eyes. *"Miigwech,"* he says, and steps back to his place in the circle. David opens the squeaky door and grabs the closest seat. Roberta smiles at him and offers the smudge. Shane looks around the room to keep from making eye contact with David. Roberta has posted new inspirational messages and help-line numbers from the Aboriginal Suicide Prevention Strategy since the last time Shane was in here. *Too little, too late,* he thinks.

David sits back down on the other side of the circle. Tara fingers the zipper on her green hoodie. Kyle and Ashley hold hands a few seats away. Shane has a lifetime of memories with all the kids assembled around the circle. They might not all be friends or even like one another much, but it would be hard to find people who know one another better. They've pulled one another's hair and slept in one another's beds. They've gone ice fishing, played video games, and built forts in the bush. They've been bored in church and sweated out their pain in ceremony. They've seen puberty stretch out gangly bodies, and in a time before shyness they compared their first pubic hairs. Some of their moms were even pregnant together. How many times has he sat in circles like this? It's a comfort and a cage.

"No one? Nobody has anything to say?" asks Roberta.

Shane snaps to attention. He hasn't been listening. Roberta's eyes scan over the faces around the circle. Most of the kids are looking at their shoes or their hands.

Roberta raises a beaded feather in her hand. "This is our last circle for Destiny, but we can end early if none of you want to talk."

Shane and the others glance around the circle. No one wants to be the first to talk.

"And then what?" Shane asks.

Roberta leans forward and holds the feather out for Shane to take. The feather shivers in the air, just out of his reach. But he doesn't have anything to say. Nothing that would make anyone feel better. Nothing that wouldn't make everyone realize it was his fault, and definitely nothing that would bring Destiny back. Shane shakes his head and leans back in his chair.

"You sure? You haven't had much to say during our circles."

Shane tries to give her a look of encouragement, something that will show her he's doing okay, but the best he can manage is a dead-eyed stare.

Roberta waits for a moment, then looks around the room. This is her weakness. If a kid says they want to do something, chances are Roberta and the others will be 100 percent behind them. But in times like this, when the fully broken reality of life is standing up in the middle of the room and making them feel like maybe the best they can hope for is to live a life just like that of their parents, that's when Roberta and the others start to crack. It's like watching the thick ice on the lake bust up in spring, except with Roberta there's nothing underneath. No life-giving lake, just terror and good intentions. It makes some kids think that maybe it's not worth trying at all. It makes them think that maybe the game is rigged and the only way to win is by giving up. It makes some kids believe in the deepest parts of themselves that suicide is the loudest and strongest statement they can make. The only one anyone will hear.

Roberta looks at Shane, pleading with him. The only difference between the adults and the kids is that the adults have been around longer so they've survived more loss. Which is something. But it's not enough.

"What's the point of this?" Kyle asks, addressing the tiles between his feet. Shane stiffens. Kyle is the last person he needs to hear right now. Roberta passes the feather to Kyle. Kyle hesitates for a moment, then takes it. "My cousin Jared killed himself last year. People kill themselves all the time. Nobody cares till they're dead." It's true. Jared died just over a year ago, and here they are again. Kyle turned into a more or less decent person for six months after, but it didn't last.

Roberta nods her head gravely. "Mmm. Sometimes it's hard to know when people care. But let's try to stay away from blame. We're all here for each other."

Kyle pushes on. "But, like, why are we here now? Why didn't we have a circle for Destiny or Jared when they were still alive?"

Shane glowers at Kyle, willing him to shut up.

"Somebody had to know, right?" Kyle looks at Shane. "Normal sixteen-year-old girls don't just—"

"Shut up, Kyle!" David says. Roberta puts out a hand, warning David against speaking when he doesn't have the feather.

"But Shane's right here!"

Roberta holds out her hands again. "David, Kyle is speaking now. You may not like what he has to say, but it's his turn to talk."

Kyle tilts back in his chair and glances over at Shane. By this point Shane's whole body is sweating with the effort to stay in his seat. Blood rushes in his ears. The voices sound far away.

Kyle continues. "Yeah, well, as I was saying before I was rudely interrupted ... if Destiny was my little sister she would never have—"

Shane's foot hooks the leg of Kyle's chair and yanks it out from under him. Kyle cracks the back of his head against the linoleum. Shane jumps out of his chair and throws his fist at Kyle, stopping just millimeters away from his face. Shane holds his fist in place, vibrating on the edge of attack.

*

Crack, crack, crack, crack, crack, crackcrackcrackcrackcrackcrack ...

The sound of Shane's feet digging into the gravel is like the blade of a boat's motor, churning up the ground and blasting his way past the houses and shacks he's seen every day for so long that even when he closes his eyes to dream they're still there, burned in like a brand. Tara's cousin Harold moved to the city and got a brand on his arm that said: NDN PWR. It was red, angry, perfect. *What would it be like to choose the pain that marks you?* Some people say that before you're born, when you're still in the sky world, you pick the family you want to grow up with, the community you want to live in, and the things that will happen in your life. Shane liked that idea until he caught his fifth-grade teacher touching Annalise down by the water after school one day. Annalise never said a word to Shane and he never asked, even though he knew he should have. The teacher nearly fell apart trying to get Shane to stay quiet. But as much as the teacher hated himself, he must have hated Annalise more. Or maybe he just didn't care. Maybe he saw her as nothing more than a stick of kindling to be burned. But if he had grown up here, he would know that even a stick of firewood is filled with a spirit that can't be burned away.

So the next time Roberta or some other wet-eyed and well-intentioned person told Shane that everyone gets to choose the things that will happen in their lives while they're in the sky world, he remembered Annalise and the teacher and thought: *Who in the fuck would choose any of this?*

*

Shane isn't running anymore, but his lungs are on fire and his head feels like it might float away. He looks around to get his bearings. Blue corrugated aluminum siding. An ad for Sago tobacco. Gas pumps. The Dumpster. The store. *Okay.* He's outside the store. *Now why am I here?*

Shane takes a step into the back lot. In spite of his work the other day, it's still a mess. His mom always says that things look worse before they start looking better. The problem is, you never know where the turning point is going to be. *Is this the part when it gets better, or is it still going to get worse?* When Shane left he thought he had made good headway, but the yard is definitely in the "looking worse" phase. Shane pulls on a pair of baggy work gloves and yanks at a ribbon of tough black plastic that the ground behind the store has been working at reclaiming. He leans back, using his weight to pull against it. The plastic comes out of the ground in jerks and pops, flipping up clods of dirt.

"You're back."

Shane spins around at the sound of Janice's voice. One glance tells him this isn't going to be a friendly visit. "Yeah. I thought I'd put a couple hours in."

Janice takes a pull on the cigarette that never seems to leave her lips. "Got something that you want to tell me?"

Shane figures it's safest to play dumb. Who knows what this is about. "Not really. Same shit different day. You know."

"Nothing?"

Shane wipes sweat from his lip and shakes his head.

Janice frowns. "You take some sheet metal from over there?

Ah—there it is. Shane looks down at the ground, trying to remember the last time he was in genuine shit with anyone other than his uncle.

"You can't do that, Shane."

"It was by the garbage. I didn't think you would care." Shane yanks hard at the snaking ribbon of plastic in his hands. The other end pops out of the ground and gooses Janice from behind. Janice yelps and jumps about a foot in the air, which, for a woman who exercises about as often as she eats a green salad, is really something. Shane stifles a smile as Janice reaches out to retrieve her smoke from the dirt. When she rises up again, her face is redder than normal. *This can't be good.*

"Sorry, Janice."

Janice plugs the cigarette back into her mouth. "You bet you're sorry. I'm gonna have to let you go."

"Why? For some scrap that was just rusting to shit back here? I can pay you back if you really want."

"That's not the point."

"Feels like the point to me."

Janice takes a long drag on her smoke. It's almost down to the filter. Shane doesn't have long to change her mind.

"I have nothing else, Janice. I need the money."

Janice takes an envelope out of her inside pocket and passes it to Shane. "The ladies at the church took up a collection for you and your mom."

Shane looks. Small bills are crowded into a wad. It looks like a couple hundred bucks, three if he's lucky. "Thanks. This doesn't really get me anywhere but ..."

Ashley opens up the side door and pokes her head out. "Janice, the till's stuck again."

"Just give it a smack."

"I already did."

Janice shakes her head and flicks the butt of her cigarette into the yard. She tosses Shane a "Good luck," and turns her back, looking more than a little relieved to be going back inside.

Shane kicks the dirty snake of black plastic and shoves the money into his pocket. Before he goes, he grabs a few more pieces of sheet metal. He doesn't need them, but it'll piss Janice off and that's good enough for now. As he drags the sheets away, his phone buzzes with a text message from Debbie: *Come by if you wanna work.*

CHAPTER SIXTEEN

Roberta is the smartest, kindest, best person, but she doesn't have a clue. I asked her once about what kind of school I would have to do to help kids like she does. Eight more years of school, she told me. Eight! And she still doesn't have any idea how to help us. Me neither, but I didn't go to school. She handed out these cheesy sheets today that were written like legal contracts where we promised to call Roberta or our "buddy" if we're ever thinking about killing ourselves. Right. Nice idea but I don't think a little sheet of paper is going to do much if somebody wants to go through with it. Shane had taken off by then so creepy Kyle jumped in to be my "suicide buddy." Ugh. No thanks.

I love that Roberta is here though. Even if she doesn't solve anything, I like to imagine her going to school down south year after year, dreaming of doing good and caring enough to come back and try. It helps to know that. It really does.

It makes me wish I was strong enough to do something someone could look up to. But I don't think people get very much out of poems. You can't eat a poem. It won't keep you warm. It's not going to filter the water or keep kids from being taken into care. But I keep thinking that a really good one—the right magic combination of words— might save your life.

Roberta asked us to make a list of ten things that, no matter what happens, make life worth living. I only came up with four.

1. Books.
2. Writing.
3. Shane.
4. The possibility of seeing my mom again.

CHAPTER SEVENTEEN

A crow hops along the ditch in front of Shane, calling out to no one in particular, like a kid yelling at a video game. He scans the low clouds that hang like damp laundry, warning of a storm that won't come until tonight.

David's voice calls out from behind him. "Shane!"

Shane glances back, but doesn't slow his pace.

"Just tell me you're okay and I'll leave you alone," David calls.

Shane stops. All the possible responses arrive simultaneously in a hopeless jumble. Saying nothing is better than saying the wrong thing. Shane starts to walk again.

"Where are you going?"

Shane raises the cup of coffee in his hand. "Debbie's."

"Uh ... why? It's daytime."

"I might do some work for her." Shane can't muster the courage to meet David's eyes. He never talks about it, but everyone knows the reason David's parents aren't on the rez anymore is because Debbie got them hooked on opiates and they wound up on the street down in Thunder Bay.

"You can't do that."

"Do you really not get how fucked I am right now? I'm still registered for my dad's band, and they won't fund me because I live here. Our band won't fund me until I officially switch over, and they've already spent the money for this September. There might have been a way to make it work, at least to get started in Toronto if I spent my inheritance from my dad. But our roof is rotten and mold is everywhere. The band won't pay to fix it, and my uncle expects me to blow my inheritance on roofing supplies because school is useless for Indians anyways."

"Can't Roberta do anything?" David asks.

"She's doing it but it sounds like she's planning for next year now. Which means I'm stuck for a year and who knows what other shit is going to happen between now and then?"

"Why didn't you tell me?"

"Because you want me to stay. Even if I'm miserable."

David doesn't argue. Shane starts walking again. Leaving David behind feels like a cloud has passed over the sun. It's cooler without him. After a few moments, Shane hears footsteps behind him.

"I'm coming with you," David says.

"Fine. Just don't screw this up for me." He glances at David and smiles in spite of himself.

*

When they step onto Debbie's property, Shane's mouth goes dry and his chest tightens like a drum held over a fire. He's been here plenty of times, but only just to hang out or grab a bottle of something. The ramshackle buildings look different in the daylight, spread out over the property like a disease. He doesn't see Debbie at first. She would be perfectly camouflaged if her garish red lips weren't there to draw attention to the round gray stone of her face floating in the middle of the silver-planked porch.

"That coffee for me?"

Shane nods.

"Good boy." Debbie cocks her head at David. "Haven't seen you in a while." David opens his mouth as if to say something, then closes it again.

Shane jumps in. "You wanted to see me?"

Debbie leans back in her chair. "I heard you and your mom aren't doing so good."

"We're fine."

"Still, I bet you could use some cash."

Shane shrugs. "Maybe." Debbie narrows her eyes like she's trying to make up her mind about something. He feels it like a shiver along his back.

Debbie smiles, apparently satisfied. "If you get caught selling, that's it for you, you know. No more school."

"How much could I make?"

"Up to you. If you're smart and you work hard, anything's possible."

Shane nods. "Why me though?"

"Fishing for compliments?" Debbie grins. "People say you're quick. I could use some brains around here, simple as that."

Shane catches this kid Robbie out of the corner of his eye. He moves along the edge of the clearing that borders the compound, pausing like a deer that's sniffing the air for danger.

Debbie calls out to him. "Get your ass over here! Your mom told me you would be here half an hour ago!" Robbie clambers up the porch steps.

"Gimme a sec." Debbie slides off her stool and walks toward the corner, her gumball-pink sandals flapping wetly on the undersides of her feet. She crouches down and opens the safe behind the counter. Debbie's collage of the dead rises up on the wall behind her. It features Debbie's brother Ross, who hung himself; Andrea, the funny big-nosed girl who disappeared after a bush party; Annie-Mae and all her friends who were in the back of the pickup when it rolled one night; Grace, the girl with Down's who mysteriously got pregnant and then even more mysteriously fell through the ice; Makwa, the one everybody called "it" because the doctors called her a boy when she was born but she fought it until the day they found her strangled in an alley; Greg, the young guy who people said was born angry, who got shot by police in Toronto; and Destiny. The sweet-and-sour little bundle that he loved more than anything in the world, found at the end of a rope. *Stolen.*

Debbie flip-flops back to Robbie, who passes her a bill and a fistful of change in exchange for a little baggie. "All right now, get outta here before your mom calls me looking for you." Robbie skitters over the scattered gravel in the yard and disappears into the trees. Debbie pulls a package out from under her arm and holds it out for Shane.

"I did this up for you."

Shane glances from the package to David. "How old is Robbie now?" Shane asks.

"I don't know … twelve, thirteen …"

Shane shakes his head. Debbie rolls her eyes.

"Don't be like that," Debbie says. "If I wasn't selling to these kids, somebody else would. At least with me people know what they're getting. Nothing's cut with scary shit, the pills are all brand-name. None of that knock-off garbage from China or Mexico."

"I'm sure the elders are glad to know they've got you to look out for the youth," David says.

Debbie flaps her hands in the air like a couple of hand puppets. "Blah, blah, blah, I ain't even hearing you." Debbie slides the package across the counter toward Shane. "Price list is in the bag. You bring me the cash in under two weeks and I'll hand over your cut."

Shane catches David's eye. David points his lips to the clearing; they can still walk away. Shane eyes the package warily, then picks it up. It takes everything Shane has not to follow when David turns and walks down the driveway without a word.

After a moment Debbie folds her arms. "We good?"

Shane is planted in place; it feels like he'll be trapped in this spot, held in this second forever. But time continues to tumble forward as always.

"We're good." Shane wanders down the porch steps and into the clearing that surrounds the compound.

Debbie calls after him, "Hey! Put that shit away."

Shane looks down at the bag from Debbie like he forgot he's carrying a bomb. He scans the area for anyone watching, then shoves the bag into his backpack. Debbie chuckles to herself as he heads into the bush and down the hill.

There is no sign of David when Shane gets to the main road. It might be better that he's gone. Shane can think more clearly on his own. If David were here he would feel guilty about taking the bag from Debbie, but now alone, he can admit that the beating in his chest isn't all fear. There's excitement in him too. Maybe even the beginning of a kind of happiness. If this is what it takes to get him to Toronto—to a real education and freedom and options and a bit of anonymity for him and David for once in their lives— it's worth it. David is against it now, but he'll appreciate it once Shane has some money in his pocket. He'll feel different when it's happening for real.

Shane reaches into his backpack and fingers the bag from Debbie. There are the hard little lumps of pills, crunchy larger pieces of weed, and something else that feels like tiny pebbles, each in their separate baggies. This stuff may not be good for anyone, but it is *powerful*. It vibrates beneath his fingertips. And even though its darkness gets under people's skin and eats away at them, even though it turns them against one another, even though it starves and it kills, Shane can't help enjoying the shiver of pleasure that comes from having that kind of power in his hands.

He tries to remember if Debbie said anything about how much he would make from a bag like this. It's going to be more than he would ever make cleaning up at the store, that's for sure. He can go through the price list and count it up when he gets home. Shane hefts the bag in his hand to feel its weight. It isn't heavy, but it's almost as good as money. And money … right now money is the only thing standing between him and the rest of his life. This bag of poison is the closest thing to a real answer that Shane has had in a long time. *So fuck it*. David will understand eventually.

Lyndahl waves at Shane from down the street. He's all long legs and elbows, impossible to mistake for anyone else at any distance. Sweat springs from Shane's forehead without warning. He wasn't even hot until a second ago. Lyndahl is walking in the direction of Debbie's place, but there's no way to be sure where he's going without asking him directly. Shane thinks back to the times they've hung out. *Did he ever have a joint in his mouth? Did he talk about getting high on other stuff? How do you even bring that up?* Shane waves back at Lyndahl and decides that, no matter what happens, he's going to try to make a sale. Lyndahl is a nice guy; he'll be good about it even if he doesn't want anything.

"Hey, College," Lyndahl says. He grins at Shane in that sweet, lazy way he has. "Where you headed?" he asks.

Shane looks at Lyndahl's eyes. They might be a little bit red, but he could just as easily be imagining it. "Headed home. You?"

Lyndahl glances up the street. "Just walking, you know."

"Going to Debbie's?"

Lyndahl shrugs. "Maybe."

This is it. This is the moment. He should say, *You don't need to go that far. I'm selling for her now.* He should open his bag and show him what his options are. Tell him it's all good—none of it's cut with anything—that's what Debbie said. Shane stands there bobbing his head like an idiot, trying to get the words out.

"Later, College." Lyndahl's sleepy eyes slide past Shane. The cuffs of Lyndahl's jeans rasp along the road as he saunters away.

*

Shane sneaks quietly into the house. There is almost no chance that Jackie will notice or care what he's up to, but the habit of softening his footsteps and muffling the click of the door when he's doing something wrong is hard to break. One night about six months after he and David first started fooling around, Shane told David that he wanted to tell his family that he might be gay. *If you do that,* David said, *I'll never talk to you again.* That stopped the conversation for a long time, but since Destiny died, coming out has felt inevitable.

Shane came home late that night. Through the window, he could see that Jackie was waiting up for him. She was bent over her beading with her lips pressed together so hard the edges of her mouth were white. She looked up when he opened the door, and he broke down. Couldn't even keep it together long enough to get his shoes off. His mother held his hot face in her hands and kissed his wet cheeks. She only asked once what had happened, but that only made him cry harder. Because he couldn't say. That was the whole point. If he said anything, he would lose David. But if he didn't say anything, he was afraid that this love he had never felt before would choke and die of neglect. Or worse, turn into something bitter.

That night when Jackie held him and let him cry without saying a word, without asking or demanding anything of him, that night it felt like her love was forever. But he needs his mom tonight just as much as he ever did, and where is she? Here and not here. Lost.

Shane snaps the desk lamp on and tosses the bag from Debbie on top of a sheaf of papers. Time to think strategy. He can't deal out of his house. Even if his mom doesn't catch on, he can't imagine selling here. Some things are just wrong. The community center would figure it out in no time, so that place is out too. People are used to going straight to Debbie's if they want something, so if he's going to be successful, he has to go to them. He should probably have something on him at all times so he can sell when people see him too. But how much should he carry? Does he need cash so he can make change? And what about security? Does he need to carry a knife or something in case someone tries to jump him for it? He doesn't usually lock the door at home; should he start doing that too? What if someone breaks in and they can't find what they're looking for? Would they go after his mom? It isn't right. Nothing about this is right. Shane's breath comes faster. A prickling starts in his fingers and moves up his arms.

The chainsaw buzz of Shane's phone cuts through the room. He picks it up without checking who it is. "Hello?"

"Hey."

"Hey. Who's this?" Shane asks.

"What? It's me. Tara. Are you okay?"

"Yeah. I'm fine. I'm just figuring some stuff out. Did Ashley tell you I saw Debbie today?"

"No, I didn't hear. Like, you're working for her now?"

"Yeah."

"That's great. I mean it sucks, but it's money, right?"

"You don't think I should feel bad?" It was surprising how pragmatic she could be sometimes.

"No. People make their own decisions. You can't blame yourself if people want to get fucked up. I've never spent money on it, but you know I'll do stuff if people offer it. If it makes me feel like shit it's my own fault."

"It's not right though." There is silence for a moment. He can feel her getting impatient. She doesn't like it when he seems uncertain.

"It's not about right and wrong. It's about making that money and getting your ass to school," Tara says.

"Yeah." They talk for a while after that, but they don't have much to say. They exchange the same old words about missing each other and Shane promises to call her once he makes his first sale. She doesn't say I love you, and neither does he.

Shane hangs up the phone. He can hear other kids his age whooping and calling out to each other down the road. Their voices are thin and faraway sounding, like they're coming to him on a toy phone made of tin cans and string. He can't tell if they're laughing or crying for help. Nothing to be done either way. Shane imagines planting David and Jackie and Tara and all the people he's ever loved deep into the soil, with only their heads poking out. A human garden. He could feed them and talk to them and make sure nothing bad ever happened again.

An idea brushes over Shane's neck like a gray spider. He's being watched. Shane twists around to get a look at the room. Everything looks normal but it feels like someone has replaced each of his things with an exact duplicate of the original. And now if he were to walk out into the house he would see that the living room, the TV, the kitchen, even Destiny's room and his mother asleep inside have all been swapped out for identical but slightly wrong versions of themselves. Or maybe it's him. Maybe everyone else is exactly the same, and he's the one that's been exchanged for another version of himself, one that's attracted to guys, one that sees spirits and deals drugs to teenagers.

Shane shoves the bag of pills and powders and weed into the back of his desk drawer. He should make a list of people he can sell to, and then hide one small baggie of each drug in the small compartments of his backpack. He should find a permanent hiding place for the rest. That would be smart. But he calls David instead.

Shane puts the phone to his ear and feels a flush of pleasure until he remembers that he's on David's shit list. David picks up but he doesn't say anything.

"David?" There's nothing but the light hiss of air on the line. "I miss you. I'm sorry," Shane says. The words fizz from Shane's phone up to a satellite in space, and then beam back down to David. They travel tens of thousands of kilometers to be heard a fifteen-minute walk away. "I'm sorry about the shit with Debbie. I wish I knew another way ... maybe I could just sell to older people or ..."

"People that don't matter?"

"I don't know what to do, David."

"I know."

"Do you?"

"No."

The hissing silence passes between them, connecting them like an umbilical cord. He imagines that he can hear David's breathing, the warm steady beat of his heart. Imagines him with the Toronto guidebook in his lap, its words and pictures fluttering on the backs of his eyelids like gray birds reflected in a stream.

"I—" A loud crack comes from the other side of the bedroom door. It's followed by a sound like a bathtub full of chunky stew getting dropped in the living room. Jackie calls for him from Destiny's room. Shane opens the door and pokes his head down the hall. The living room is awash in rotten drywall and swampy water. The bulging area around the leak has become a gaping hole in the ceiling. Shane realizes he's still holding the phone.

"Oh shit! Sorry David—I have to call you back."

*

Cleaning the place up takes most of the night, and when he's done no one would really call it livable. He does what he can, but the living room is finished. The smell is so bad he has to run out for air a few times to keep from throwing up. Shane finds some old plastic drop sheets under the sink and staples them to the door frame. At least that way Jackie won't wander in. *Good thing it's summer. But what happens next time it rains?*

He closes the door of his bedroom. Through the window, he can see the light beginning to brighten the treetops outside. He collapses into bed and pulls the blankets up around his chin. The room seems deadly quiet at first, and then the little sounds of life creep in like they're being turned up by a remote control. Cue the distant rumble of the train. Cue the *crack* of gravel under a truck's tires. Cue the lapping of waves and the friendly sound of boats nuzzling the dock.

Shane rolls over on his side and checks his phone for messages. He sees one from David: *Come over tomorrow morning. My* nookomis *wants to see you.* Shane sighs. It's already morning. He sees that David sent another message ten minutes later: *I <3 you.*

Shane wants to roll over and ignore it, but something bubbles up in him and won't allow him to put the phone down. His fingers hover over the screen for a painfully long moment. Shane silently counts, *One … two … three … four … five …*

When he's done counting and the kicking in his chest has

settled into a sickening sway, Shane types: *I <3 you more.* He slides the phone across the floor to the other side of the room. Maybe that way he won't be tempted to check it every five seconds. Maybe. Shane shimmies under the covers and turns out the light. There's a grizzly on his chest and minnows in his stomach, but he can't stop smiling.

CHAPTER EIGHTEEN

She might be lying but Ashley's auntie Lisa said she saw my mom when she was out in Dryden a few weeks ago. She told Ashley that she asked if my mom was going to come back to visit my dad and me. She said my mom laughed, like it was funny that me and my dad might want to see her. Lisa said my mom was just passing through town, only there for one night. She said she's lost weight and she's blond now. Dryden's a shit hole, but it's only about an hour away. After leaving without a word for years, she couldn't drive for even an hour. What did I do to her? Roberta says it doesn't have anything to do with me, but that's bullshit. It has to have something to do with me. Even if she left for her own reasons, she left me here with him. She left knowing that it would hurt me. That's why people don't just leave their kids. They don't just walk away. It's too cruel. There has to be a reason. It's messed up, but I would rather believe that I did something to drive her away than just shut up and accept the fact that the people I love and trust might just walk away for no reason at all. That can't be true. I couldn't handle it.

Shane is no better. People say I'm lucky to have him taking care of me, but that's bullshit. I'm the one that's been propping him up when he's sad, worrying about what might happen to the plans for his *future. And then when I get the first news I've had about my mom in years and it's SHITTY, he can't even be bothered to ask me what's wrong. I end up helping HIM. Reassuring HIM. Telling him it's okay to be a drug dealer if you're doing it for a good reason. I love him but sometimes I want to scream,* You have it so easy! People believe in you! They want you to succeed! Man up!

I wanted to write a poem or something more about Mom, but I don't have anything left. I don't even hate her anymore. I feel like she's something awful that happened to someone I used to know.

CHAPTER NINETEEN

When Shane steps outside, he is reminded how a good rain refreshes the world. Most of the world, anyway, not his crappy little house. It's like the laws of the universe reverse themselves as soon as you cross the threshold. Rain leads to rot. Roofs let the weather in. Daughters die before mothers. Sons take care of mothers. Each breath he takes in the outside air is a relief. Even though he barely slept and he doesn't know why Evie asked him to come over, stepping outside the mushroomy walls of his house feels like a small taste of freedom.

Last night Shane dreamed that he was standing in the middle of the house with his arms stretched up to the ceiling, barely supporting the weight of the place on his palms. His arms shuddered and shook. He called out to his mom and David, who sat at opposite ends of the table picking dry husks out of a basket of *manomin*. *Help me! I need your help!* he called. Jackie and David stayed hunched over the basket, absorbed in their task. They bowed their heads and said in unison, *You have all the help you need.* That's all he remembers. As if there wasn't enough uncertainty in Shane's life, his dreams never have clear borders and they never really end. They stop before anything is resolved: all questions and no answers.

*

Evie's house sits a little ways back from the road behind a fringe of trees. It was built and maintained by generations of men who were lucky enough to get steady work nearby. Unlike most families, they were able to maintain the old ways through the decades when it was illegal to sweat or drum or speak the language. Their rebellion is the only reason those ways weren't lost forever.

Shane stands in front of Evie's house, not yet ready to go in and unable to walk away. The screen door squawks. Evie comes out drying her hands with a red cloth. She looks down and squints at Shane standing by the road. He freezes on the spot, gripped by the idea that maybe Evie, like some ancient creature from one of her stories, won't be able to see him if he doesn't move.

Evie squints harder. "Shane?"

He lets out a breath. "I thought you were pretty much blind."

"Blind maybe, but not stupid." Evie grins. "C'mere and help me shake this out."

*

Inside, Evie shuffles around the kitchen with a kettle of hot water. Shane slouches in a cracked wooden chair. "Is David here?"

"Oh, he's around somewheres." Evie sets her battle-scarred teapot down on the table beside Shane and settles into her chair with the dusty-rose cushion. Shane reaches out for the teapot and pours them both some tea, hoping David will come soon. His eyes follow the steam billowing from his cup. He knows if he were to turn his head, she would be squinting hard at him over the top of her thick lenses.

"How's your mom?" Evie asks at last.

Is this why he's here? "You should ask her."

Evie frowns and blows little gusts of air over the surface of her tea, sending up wispy puffs of steam that fog her glasses

"You got time to pick *manomin* later today? I was supposed to go out with David but my bum leg won't let me."

"You never missed going out on the water in your life."

Evie nods. "That's what happens when you get old. First time for everything. And at my age there aren't a lot of first times left, so I better make the best of it." Evie smiles.

Shane nods. "I, um … I could use some cash. For school in Toronto." *Jesus, this is embarrassing. You don't ask an elder for money when they want you to help them.*

Evie frowns. "You'd be more good to us if you stayed here. Bad things happen when people go down south. They get a degree, get addicted, go gay, and who knows what else. We don't hardly see them after."

Shane takes a long swig of tea. "A hundred bucks?" He can't believe he's doing this.

Evie stares him down, giving him that elders' look. The one that usually means *You're in deep shit.* Shane's belly does a flip. There's still time to apologize or play it off as a joke. She wouldn't believe him but …

"Seventy-five," Evie says.

Shane strokes his beardless chin and makes a show of thinking about it. "Deal. You're gonna have so much rice you won't know what to do."

They chat for a while longer, sipping their tea and avoiding any talk about Jackie. It's not long before David comes in from the yard with some rough tarpaulin bags and firewood.

"You made it."

"I did." Shane smiles. He wishes he could say, *You look good with a stick of wood in your hands!* But he doubts David's grand-mother would laugh at that one.

Evie is in the kitchen struggling with a jar of pickles. "David, gimme some help with this." David takes the sweaty jar in his hands and twists at the lid. It resists for a moment, then it makes that satisfying little sucking sound and pops open.

"How does it look out there?"

"Great. Clear sky. Flat water."

"Good." Evie picks up a slice of bologna and chews it thought-fully. "So Shane, when you going to get my grandson a pretty little girlfriend like yours?"

Shane laughs. "I think that's up to him."

"Leave love up to young men and it'll never happen."

Shane and David exchange sly smiles.

"You've been seeing a lot of each other lately."

David turns red. Shane pours himself some more tea.

Evie squints at them. "You know, it's good to have other young men as friends. Not too close, though. Too much male energy is no good. There has to be balance."

The air in the kitchen is suddenly thick. Shane and David don't dare to risk another look at each other.

"I know," David says.

"Yeah, that's right," Shane agrees. "I'll ask Tara if she has any friends that might have a crush on David." He resists the urge to glance at Evie to get a sense of how much she's picking up on, and how much is coincidence. Shane can tell David is trying hard to make it look like he's focusing on getting a slippery pickle out of the jar, but there's not much that gets past his grandmother.

Evie frowns. Shane stands up before she can ask another question.

*

It's just like David said, open and clear, a perfect day to be on the water. They walk to the lake side by side. Each time David's hand bumps against Shane's the crackle of their secret dances up and down his body. Like a bird flying against a strong wind, they may not be going anywhere but at least they're flying.

Shane's phone buzzes. Tara is messaging him again. She's been at it all morning but Shane doesn't know how to respond. *Where RU? U OK?*

Shane wishes he could write back, *Why can't I just do my own thing sometimes without you getting in my face?* But of course he doesn't. Shane types: *On way to the islands with David. Back by dark.* That should satisfy her for a while. He turns the phone off and stashes it away in his bag again, knowing there will be a storm of messages coming through from Tara when he turns it back on again.

Shane and David push their way through tall grasses that chastise them like frustrated librarians. *Shhhhhhh! Shhhhhhh!*

Shhhhhhh! David's arm grazes Shane's, lingering long enough that he imagines he can feel the meshing of the fine hairs along their arms before David pulls away again. Shane grins at David.

"Don't look at me like that. Someone's gonna see." David's eyes scan the field.

Shane won't be shut down. "So you heart me, hey?"

David smiles a shy, little-boy smile.

"I heart you too."

David laughs. "Brave. Very brave."

"We can say it with the real word if you want." Shane casts a sly glance David's way. Should he push it? Loose hair dangles in front of David's eyes, making him impossible to read. "I can even say it first," Shane ventures.

"*Heart's* good for now." David pushes aside a clump of tall purple thistles, letting the grasses do the talking for him. *Shhhhhhh! Shhhhhhhhh! Shhhhhhhhh!* Shane gives him a good-natured shove and follows him, replaying their exchange in his mind, trying to figure out what just happened. David didn't say he loved him, but he didn't take back his text either. It could have been a brush-off, or a lead-up to an *I love you*, or anything at all.

*

David gives the engine some gas, and they putter slowly away from the dock. Once they're clear of the bay, David guns the motor, nearly sending Shane tumbling into his lap. Shane grabs on to the side of the boat and pulls himself upright again. David laughs.

The front end of the little aluminum boat rises off the surface of the water. Shane imagines it lifting higher and higher until they are up over the bristling tops of the trees. But where would they go? Is there anywhere more beautiful than this? Anything better than the two of them with the prospect of a long afternoon alone together, bodies warming in the sun …

David turns the boat at an angle, and a rush of cold water hits Shane full in the face. "Got to pay attention on the water," David yells. "You never know what's going to happen!" David's cackle rises up over the roar of the engine and he turns the boat toward the shore. Shane does his best to dry off with the hem of his T-shirt, but it's wet too.

David cuts the motor and they drift into a quiet corner of the lake, where there's an old wooden shack by the water. It's the house Evie's mother was born in, but no one has lived there for years. "Gotta pick up the canoe. *Nookomis* likes to keep it close to the rice."

"Why do we need the canoe? You've got a boat."

"*Nookomis* says she can taste the gas in the rice. Prop gets caught up in it too." They pull the boat up onshore and drag the old fiberglass canoe to the water. They don't need much, just paddles, a few bags for the rice, and a pair of wooden knockers.

*

When they get to the narrow canal that leads to the mouth of the creek, David stops paddling. The long green stalks of rice wade into the lake like a crowd of elegant, willowy women. They dip their heavy heads in the breeze and graze the surface of the water with the tips of their leaves. Shane's eyes travel up the snaking line of the creek with its lean banks and mossy shoulders. Wet, abundant life ripples through the water and the trees, filling the landscape with a hum of sex and bugs and honey. It flashes bright green in the water; it rattles through the air like a chorus of singers calling him into their song. The voice of this place tugs at something buried beyond memory—an aching need as basic as thirst. His body swells with life.

"Look at all this." David's arms sweep open to embrace it all. "Couple of lucky neechees, hey?"

Shane nods. *Lucky.*

They pick up their paddles and push deeper into the rice. Shane sits at the front of the canoe, slowly pulling them through the marsh, while the heads of rice nod above them. David sits in the back, humming and clacking the sticks in time to a powwow song that Shane only half-remembers. He'd like to join in, but it makes him shy to admit when he doesn't know the traditional stuff. It feels like he should have been born knowing it. David keeps singing and gently pulls the rice toward the canoe and taps along the stalk. Long green grains drop into the bottom of the canoe with a soft rattle like rain on dry leaves.

*

Shane and David lie together, hidden in the lengthening shadows of the high grass. The sun sinks low, throwing lurid splashes of color over the water. David leans down and brushes a stem of rice over Shane's cheek.

Shane closes his eyes. "Tell me a story."

David traces the shape of Shane's eyelids with the fine whiskers of the *manomin*. "I've been thinking about our ancestors.

Where we came from. *Nookomis* says that the Anishinaabe originally lived on the east coast. But they left everything to come here when a prophet told them it was their destiny to move until they reached the place where food grows upon the water." David taps Shane's nose with the rice. "It's the *manomin* that told them they were home."

"I've heard that before."

"Can you imagine? Leaving everyone and everything you've known for the vague promise of something that you don't even know exists? Crazy."

Shane doesn't know what to say. "What do you think I'm trying to do with school?"

David furrows his brow like he doesn't understand or doesn't want to hear. Shane continues. "It's not really a prophecy, but I've been told my whole life that if I want to get an education and do something meaningful, I have to leave. Whether they're right or not, I have to try."

"It's still different."

"Is it? I bet there were Anishinaabe back in the day who thought the prophecy was stupid, who thought they were idiots to go off looking for food on the water. I bet there were people who wanted to stay home and stick to their traditions."

"Even if you're right, I don't have a reason to go." David's eyes follow a bird crossing the sky.

"How about because I'm asking?"

"I'm not your dog."

Shane stiffens. David isn't even trying to understand. "Don't you want a chance to be yourself without a couple hundred pairs of eyes on you all the time?"

"I am being myself. Mostly. I don't tell everybody everything, but that doesn't mean I'm lying."

"Doesn't matter. Hiding and lying are pretty much the same."

David is quiet. The sun dips below the edge of the lake. A haze of light hangs in the air like smoke. Shane takes his hand.

David lets out a long breath. "If I come with you, it doesn't mean you're right."

A little bird flutters in Shane's chest. "Okay."

"It doesn't mean I'll stay."

Shane chooses his words carefully. "You don't have to. I might not either. I don't know what's going to happen any more than you do." Shane hesitates before asking, "What changed your mind?"

David laughs. "You used my teachings against me!"

Shane laughs too. Laughing feels good.

"If our ancestors were brave enough to leave the place they came from in order to find something that feeds them, I can give it a shot."

Shane nods. "But … ?"

"You shouldn't have to sell drugs to get us there."

"No, I shouldn't. But there's no other way. What Janice gave me from the church ladies, plus what I'm making from Evie isn't going to get us anywhere."

David thinks for a moment. "I won't help you do it."

Shane squeezes David's hand. So he's willing to come, but it's all on Shane to make it happen. Figures.

"If you're coming with me, I'm gonna need to tell Tara. It's not fair."

David's leg tenses under Shane's hand. "Just wait until we have the money."

"She deserves to know," Shane says.

"It won't be much longer."

Shane lets it go. There are only a few precious minutes of light left before they need to go home. He runs his hand up David's shirt and rests it in the small of his back. They breathe together and listen. Birds, insects, the wind rushing through leaves: the sounds of the world rise around them like the whir of a timeless machine. It eases something between them, as though all their troubles have been wrapped up in a cloud of spider silk and harmlessly suspended just out of reach.

*

Shane uses the noise of the motor as an excuse to stay quiet for the boat ride back home. It's taken a long time to get David to the point where he's even willing to talk about leaving. Shane doesn't want to push him too hard about Tara, but he can't sit around waiting for the right time much longer. There will never be a good time to hurt Tara and expose themselves. Shane leans forward in his seat and sets his eyes on the glow of home.

It's dark when they round the corner of the bay, way past sunset but too early for moonrise. David cuts the engine and lets them drift in. One bare lamppost casts a halo of greenish light from the dock like a cat's eye in the shadows. Shane jumps out of the boat and ties off the bow and stern with a rough scrap of rope. David lifts the heavy sacks of rice onto the dock.

With every step away from the lake, a chill enters the silence between them, reminding Shane that who they were out there on the water is not who they can be here. All around them, black smudges of trees form an uncertain line between the land and sky. Shane stops walking. If they can't go forward together, and it's impossible to go backward …

David adjusts one of the bags in his arms. "What?"

Shane smiles. "I'm gonna miss you."

"I'm not going anywhere."

"It's different when it's just us."

"Don't worry about right now. Once we get to Toronto, we'll be together all the time."

"Promise?"

David smiles and leans in to kiss him. Their tongues touch, and it's almost too much, like the second before you burst into the kind of laughter you can't stop. It passes between them like something sacred, like a teaching about truth that doesn't sink in until you live the goodness of it. The moon rises over the treetops, as though unable to leave Shane and David in the dark for another instant. It shines on them like a spotlight, painting traces of silver in their hair.

A *crack* of gravel goes off like a bomb. The boys whirl around and scan the shadows for the source. "Hey guys." Tara steps into the light, which only moments before had seemed like it was shining just for him and David.

Shane tries on a smile, but it twitches like a turtle flipped on its back. Shane tries to make up for it by rushing in for a quick kiss on the cheek. Tara pulls him into a hug and keeps him there. The vodka bottle in her fist presses hard against his back.

"I saw you," she whispers.

Shane tries to pull away, but she holds on to him like he's in danger. David is edging sideways like a crab, ready to make a break for it.

"Don't look at him."

"Tara, I—"

Tara loosens her arms and lets them fall to her sides. She's not even looking at him anymore. "You were kissing him! Right here."

David forces a laugh and steps forward. "Holaay, Tara, looks like you got the party started early. How much did you drink?"

"I'm not drunk!"

Shane puts his hand on her arm. "Why don't you come with us for a bit? We'll grab a 40 and talk about stuff."

Tara jerks away. "Don't touch me!"

Shane raises his hands helplessly at David, looking for help. "David, maybe we should—"

"No!"

Shane's eyes plead with him. "We talked about this."

"You said we were gonna wait," David says.

Tara's eyes are wide, looking more and more like something that's been in a cage too long. "Wait for what?"

"See, she already knows!"

Tara's hands fly to her face, and she freezes. Tears run out between her fingers.

"C'mon, we've got to get this rice home." David pulls at Shane's sleeve.

Tara speaks quietly, her hands still over her eyes. "You can't just leave me here. You have to talk to me."

David pulls at Shane again. "We gotta go. Talk to her when she sobers up."

Tara lifts her head and looks at Shane. "Why are you listening to him?"

David backs away, ready to leave with or without him. This is the moment. One way or the other. Forward or back. Home or away. Dead or alive. Shane makes a bet on the future. "I'm sorry, Tara." Shane steps away.

"Please don't leave."

"Lemme call you later?" Shane walks up the hill and away from her, knowing he's hurting Tara to help himself. Knowing he's doing the wrong thing but not knowing what the right thing to do would be. Putting one foot in front of the other until he's far enough away that he can convince himself that shoving her aside was unavoidable. When Shane looks back, all that is visible of Tara is the winking of the moonlight on her bottle between the trees.

*

They flip up their hoodies and duck their heads down, their view a mass of blurry asphalt and beat-up sneakers. It would be some kind of miracle not to bump into someone on the way back to David's. Tonight's the kind of night when the terrifying prospect of being an unknown face in the city might actually give some comfort. To know that you could stand in a group of hundreds, even thousands of people, and still be invisible.

"You should have let me tell her."

Shane watches David's profile, hoping for a word, a nod, even a change in the pace of his walk. David's face is locked up tight. Shane wonders if it is worse to lose hope in a sea of strangers, or to lose hope surrounded by the people you love the most.

*

They enter David's place through the back door, careful not to make any noise. David goes to show Evie the rice and see about getting Shane's money. Shane slips into David's bedroom unseen. He closes the door behind him, hovers in the middle of the room, feeling his wet socks seeping into the braided rug. His heart is pounding hard. Tara's face flashes in his mind. *So much pain.* Shane digs his nails into his arm to have something else—a bright kernel of hurt to focus on. Her face again: *She knows. Soon everyone will know. And no money to get away.*

The air in the room is tight, but he can't open the door. He can't make any noise.

Shane's eyes move over the walls. Small twigs of cedar are pinned above the doors and windows. A poster from Roberta hangs above David's bed. It has cheesy photographs of animals with a list of the seven grandfather teachings with descriptions of each. *Honesty, Truth, Humility, Love, Wisdom, Courage, Respect* ... A photo of Destiny sits on the nightstand smiling at him like she's asking, *What are you gonna do now, big brother?* Shane looks back at the poster and repeats the teachings to himself, spinning them into a desperate prayer: *Honesty,Truth,Humility,Love,Wisdom,Courage,RespectHonestyTruthHumilityLoveWisdomCourageRespecthonestytruthhumilitylovewisdomrespect* ...

And then Destiny is there. She's in the room, just beyond sight, beyond the reach of his fingers, but he knows that if he turns his head she'll be gone. Shane repeats the prayer again and again for as long as he can, remembering the sandpaper edges of Destiny's laugh, the little scar from her homemade lip piercing that their mom made her get fixed, the way she could never see someone cry without breaking into tears herself ...

Honesty,Truth,Humility,Love,Wisdom,Courage,RespectHones-
tyTruthHumilityLoveWisdomCourageRespecthonestytruthhumili-
tylovewisdomrespect ...

A touch behind his ear makes him turn. But of course Destiny isn't there. She's nowhere. Shane looks down. His socks are still wet from the boat. He pulls them off and grinds his toes into the rug. He used to duck his head in here to say hi when he came to get Destiny, but he has never been in David's room alone. It should feel like home, but his body won't relax. His smell is everywhere. Normally it would settle him down but right now he can't imagine looking at David without seeing Tara's face.

Honesty,Truth,Humility,Love,Wisdom,Courage,RespectHones-
tyTruthHumilityLoveWisdomCourageRespecthonestytruthhumili-
tylovewisdomrespect ...

Shane pulls open the top drawer of David's dresser and roots around for a fresh pair of socks. The glossy corner of what looks like a magazine pokes out from underneath the pile. Shane shoves the socks aside, wondering how David would have gotten his hands on a real porno magazine up here. Shane reaches inside and pulls it out, but it's not a magazine. It's the Toronto guidebook. David has highlighted sections about the city's gay village and circled the spot on the map where the Native Canadian Centre is. Shane smiles to himself and slides the book back into the drawer.

There's a creak and the sound of feet from the hallway. David slips back into the room and closes the door softly behind him. Without a word, Shane wraps his arms around David's waist and nuzzles into his neck. Seeing that book has cracked open Shane's doubt and fear, for the first time allowing him to consider that maybe loving David won't lead to more pain. Maybe lasting love between two men is possible, even if there is no one in his life to prove it. Maybe they can find a way to figure it out together. Come morning, they'll have to.

David lets out a long breath. "You're not mad at me anymore?"

Shane shakes his head.

"Do you think Tara's telling people?"

"She'll be fine. I'll go over there tomorrow and tell her everything."

"Everyone's gonna know."

Shane presses his forehead to David's. "Once we're gone, it doesn't matter what anyone else thinks." Shane pulls David close. David's lips move along the bristling hairs at the back of Shane's neck.

In a whisper so soft that Shane almost believes he's imagining it, David says, "I love you."

He's been waiting so long to hear them, the words don't feel real. He hoped it would anchor him somehow, but he's still adrift. Shane pulls back so he can see David's eyes. "I love you too," he says. And that's when it matters. Saying it makes him feel rooted, like he's finally planted his feet on solid ground.

*

Jackie's eyes dart back and forth beneath her eyelids like panicked minnows. Her head is wrenched over the arm of the couch like the stop sign in front of the store that's been bent over since Tara's dad ran into it with his truck last year. It's a wonder that she can sleep that way in the heat of summer, all bundled up like a baby on a cradleboard.

Shane runs a finger along the edge of her cheek. "Mom. You shouldn't sleep out here, Mom."

Jackie moans softly, still halfway inside the world of dreams. Shane wonders if Destiny is alive for Jackie in that place, or if it is actually worse than here in some unthinkable way.

"The phone kept ringing and ringing," Jackie says.

"Shhh … Let's get you into bed."

Jackie leans on Shane and they shuffle toward the hall. "She must have been so sad. How come we never saw how sad she was?"

CHAPTER TWENTY

Like a heel in a boot.
Like soup in a bowl.
Like a fist in a palm
You fit into me.
It burns like hell.
But I don't mind.
If you asked me I would let you
Do anything.
Open me up and crawl inside
My skin.
So I can have all of you.
Even the soft parts.
I can be your home
If it means getting more
Than just the hardest part of you.

Ignore that. I can't believe I wrote it. I can't believe
I was that stupid. All those times imagining our new life.

All that time spent worrying about how to make him love me. What a joke. He doesn't give a shit. He never did. I was like some ugly rock that he was hiding behind.

What do you do when the only person you trust enough to cry with is the person who broke your heart?

CHAPTER TWENTY-ONE

Shane lies in bed with his face pressed against the pillow. Soft light spills in through the window, palest blue. A wave of dark hair washes over his cheek. Tara. Shane lets out a long deep breath and rolls onto his back, but his eyes stay closed.

Tara whispers in his ear, "Shane. Don't wake up. It's the only way to win." He feels the soft press of her lips against his.

Shane opens his eyes. The room is empty. He throws off the covers and jumps out of bed. His breath comes in gusts, like he has been doing sprints in his sleep. A trace of Tara lingers in the room, a sweet smell that follows her even though she swears she never wears perfume.

His phone blinks from the nightstand. Shane looks at it strangely, until the memory of last night comes barreling through the room like a pickup. *She knows.* He looks at his phone: fifteen missed calls and a string of texts from Tara. He tries to imagine how she's feeling right now. But he's never had anyone leave him like that. He's never been tossed away. And she's had a lifetime of it. He gets dressed and heads out the door, trying to ignore the dull knocking of his stomach, like a pair of sneakers in the dryer.

*

Colorless gray clouds hang dangerously low, like they're pushing against the air, trying to break loose. When Shane gets to Tara's, the squat little trailer is still dark inside. No sign of life. Tara and her dad are probably sleeping it off in different corners. Shane walks through the yard and climbs the stack of boxes to her window. He raps on the glass and looks inside for the tangle of Tara's hair spread over her pillow. The room is still full of stuffed animals and crap from when they were kids, but no Tara. There's a hollow at the foot of the bed from when she last sat there.

He goes around to the front of the house and bangs on the door. If Glen can hear him, it doesn't look like he's going to answer. *This isn't good.* He walks off the property and dials Tara's cell number. It rings a few times, then goes to voice mail. He should hang up.

"Hey, Tara … I'm sorry about last night. That was messed up. I'm sorry. Call me, okay?" Shane hangs up and slides the phone into his pocket. He keeps his hand wrapped around it like a worry stone, hopeful that it will jump alive at any moment with a call or a message.

When he looks up, Tara is walking ahead of him.

"Tara!" Shane calls.

She doesn't look back. Her dark hair flaps against her hoodie like a heavy cape. Shane can't tell if she's ignoring him or if maybe she has earphones in. *Nothing about this feels right.* Tara disappears around a corner and down the gravel road that leads to the abandoned house.

"Tara!" Shane jogs up to the corner where she turned, but she's already gone. He keeps following, even though the knocking in his stomach gets louder with every step. Shane walks up the stairs carefully, pausing after each one like an old man afraid to slip on the ice. When he reaches the top, he stops to take a last breath of fresh air, then steps inside.

"Tara?" Shane listens, but there isn't any sound here. He passes through the living room. It looks like somebody had a good time last night. There're empty bottles scattered around, and the floor is still damp from where some drinks got tipped over.

Shane kicks the neck of a beer bottle, sending it spinning in lazy circles. The mouth of the bottle swings past Shane, past the front door, past the living room, the hallway. It slows down and stops, pointed toward the bedroom door. If this were a game of spin the bottle, he would have his partner.

An invisible current pulls him down the long narrow hallway. Shane takes a step forward, and then another. The scrape of his shuffling feet on the plywood floors seems louder than the last time he was here. He resists the instinct to snap his eyes shut and plug his ears. The urge to run builds with each step toward the bedroom like the pressure of a river against the gates of a dam.

When he pushes open the door, the dam breaks. A shape is hanging from the rafters. A body. A body in Tara's clothes. A body with her arms. Her legs. Her face. Her body. Tara. But there is nothing of her in it. It is a husk.

Where did she go?

*

It's hard to say how long Shane has been outside. The tingling came like the beginning of a Drift, but it didn't take him away. He was trapped there in that skeleton of a house, ripped apart and numb. Aware enough to do what he was supposed to. Dial the number. Make the call. Wait. And wait.

He's still waiting, but they're here now. The police car in front of the house has its lights on, like they want people to come and see. But when people do come, one worried face after the other, Officer Larkin holds them back and tells them to go home. Nothing to see here. *Turn off your lights,* Shane wants to say. *This isn't a circus.* They try to talk to Shane, but Larkin won't let him say anything. Shane doesn't mind. He doesn't have words anyway.

The police have him sitting on an old couch to the side of the house. Shane keeps closing his eyes and trying to set out on a Drift, but the Drift won't come. Destiny won't either. He's trapped. Alone. Waiting. Shane stares down at his runners, two dirty white wings in the mud. He grabs a rag from the couch and rubs at the black marks on the leather of his shoes. The mud smears around, making the shoes blotchy beige. Shane wonders if they've cut her down yet, or if she's still hanging there waiting to fall into some cop's arms. For the first hour, he listened for the sound of rope being sawed, of a weight being dropped, but it's been quiet so far. There's just the odd flash of their cameras lighting up the fringes of his vision.

Two cops he hasn't seen before today talk in low voices just inside the house. They stand straight, with their protective vests holding their backs flat as action figures.

"Is he still outside?"

"I told him to wait."

"Let's get him home."

One officer steps out of the house and stands with his belt at eye level with Shane.

"Shane?"

Shane lifts his head up. The officer is a dark silhouette, a smudge against the gray sky.

CHAPTER TWENTY-TWO

The old ladies have done up the bingo hall extra-nice for Tara's funeral. They had to open the sliding wall that normally separates the smoking and non-smoking sections so that they would have space for everybody. Burgundy drapes have been hung over the light-up bingo boards. The cage that holds the balls must be stashed away somewhere. Shane wonders who decided it was against the rules to look at bingo stuff during a funeral. The hall will never be pretty, so they might as well leave it as is. That would be more honest. It makes sense to him that a mixed community of Catholics and people who are bringing back the old Anishinaabe ways would hold funerals in the only place where they all worship: the United Church of Bingo.

The plain room is filled to capacity. Everyone that matters to Shane, other than his mom, is here. The air is filled with muffled sobs and murmured wishes of support. People keep coming up to him, but he can't bring himself to talk. What can he say? He bets they're all looking at him, wondering what he did wrong. Asking each other how fucked up he must be to have both his sister and his girlfriend kill themselves within a couple months of each other. That's what he's thinking anyway. Even if nobody else is.

He takes a seat near the front, hoping to get started as soon as possible so it can just be over. David has been hovering on the edge of the crowd, waiting for Shane to wave him over, give permission for him to come closer. *Not likely.* He hasn't talked to David or looked at him since he found Tara. David eventually takes the seat next to Shane, ignoring his signals. It would be sweet of him to follow him around if the two of them weren't the whole reason everyone is packed into the bingo hall with Tara's body at the front of the room. They didn't have the courage to come out a few days ago, and now that Tara's dead he's still trying to get close to Shane without being honest about who they are. It's bullshit and David knows it. If he and David had never hooked up, Tara would still be alive. Simple. No getting around it. So fuck him. Fuck him and his puppy-dog eyes and his leather medicine bag. He needs to be punished. They both do.

A priest steps up to the podium. He must be new, or maybe they pulled him in from Dryden or somewhere. When he begins to speak, the words are the same ones Shane has heard come from the throats of other men who stood up there speaking for people they'll never know: They may know grief and they sure know pity. They know that they feel bad when young Indians die, but they don't believe there's anything to be done about it. These priests, social workers, teachers, government bureaucrats, they're all gravediggers in a war zone, doing their job with efficiency and compassion, but they're convinced it's hopeless. They believe that the way things are is the way they will always be. *Indians have hard lives. Indians die young. It's sad, but it's the way of the world.* Shane can see it in their watery eyes, clinging to their damp handshakes and limp summer suits. But then again, when was the last time he really made a difference? At least he hasn't given up. Giving up is a luxury reserved for people standing on the outside looking in.

He can't make himself look at the priest. But if he turns away, David is there. And straight in front of him is Tara's school photo sitting on top of her coffin. Her *coffin*. Shane forces himself to look at it. To keep his eyes open. To stare. Tara's smile in the photo is tense, like she knows she's on display and she's doing her best to give people what they expect to see. Behind her eyes is a flash of accusation, the panic of a drowning girl. *I'm so sorry, Tara.* Then the Drift takes him like a rogue wave, knocking the breath from his lungs. His whole world flashes past him in a jumble, as though it's all been picked up and tossed into a blender. Gravel whips by, peppered with cigarette butts and flecks of wild rice. David's canoe, the Toronto guidebook, the purple curtains from Destiny's room, Kyle and Ashley swirl past hand in hand. The side of Jackie's face is visible for a moment, then gone. Shane looks up through the center of the swirling mass. Two figures float above him, just out of reach. Wind whips their hair over their faces, but there is no mistaking Tara and Destiny. Shane reaches up for Tara's ankle. His fingers stretch to their limit, as he wills his body to extend only a little bit farther. His fingertips brush the sole of Tara's shoe and he's about to grab hold of her when he feels a cold touch at his wrist.

Shane looks down. David strokes Shane's hand with two fingers, careful to make sure that no one sees. The priest is still at the front. Before Shane realizes it, his feet have carried him up the aisle and out of the hall. He can feel everyone's heads turning as he goes. They'll crane their necks to follow him out the door, then snap back around to the priest like they're all attached to the same rubber band. Once he's gone, the whispers will start.

Outside, thick clouds crowd the sky like grotesque blobs of mud. It's like the world has flipped on her back in surrender. The sky is mud and the earth is gone. How else to explain the weight on his shoulders and the lightness of his feet? The point is alive with stiff grasses that thrash with each gust of the coming storm. The sky is ready to break open at any moment. Shane slows to a walk, feeling the wind shove against him, wishing that it would rip the grasses up from their roots and take him along with it. He's sure to find life better in the sky world. Shane stops at the end of the point. His hands ache from being clenched into fists. He straightens one finger at a time, feeling the wind wick sweat from the damp creases. A paper ball drops from his right hand. It's a copy of the funeral program he's kept crushed in his fist since they handed it to him. Shane bends down to pick it up. He tries to smooth the creases in the cover, but the damage is done. It looks old, already an artifact. Shane follows the white line that cuts through the top of Tara's photo. It's the same white line that ran through the program at Destiny's funeral. Roberta must have used the same ancient printer at the back of the school office.

He pulls the pages apart. One of Tara's poems is printed inside:

Now you see me. Now you don't.
You weave me in and out of your life.
A thread worked into a hemline.
Invisible, almost.
Now you see me.

Now you don't.

Invisible is not the same as gone.

Shane lets his hand fall to his side. He tries to remember if he has ever read anything Tara wrote. Who was the "you" she was talking to—Shane or her mom? She was always scribbling in her notebook, but he never asked about it more than a couple of times, and he doesn't even remember what she said she was doing. *Girl stuff,* he probably thought. The smell of rain comes over the lake in the instant before he feels the first drop.

A voice calls to him. "Shane!"

Shane doesn't turn. There's no reason to. It's David's voice, rising over the rush of the wind and water.

"Shane!" He walks lightly over the wet mess of earth, barely making a sound. Evie says he is a good hunter. She must be right.

"Why did you leave?"

He won't turn until he has to. Why should he? It's fucked up that David came here. Today of all days, they should stay away from each other. It's the least they can do for Tara. A crack of lightning moves through Shane's body when David touches his shoulder. Shane swings around. "What? What do you want?"

David is stunned into silence. Shane can see how bad he's hurting, but he can't make himself care.

"See this?" Shane holds up Tara's memorial program. "This is on me and you."

David flinches, but he holds his ground. As if just being there is supposed to make things better somehow. Shane wants to kick him or punch him or bite him—anything to get a reaction.

Shane shoves the program hard against David's chest. "You

know what? Stay the fuck away from me." Shane plows through the matted weeds just as the real rain begins. It beats at his back, making his clothes cling to his skin. He imagines the raindrops turning into fat wads of soil and muck that pool into the streets, flowing up around his ankles and thighs, swallowing up cars and houses and babies, devouring grannies and uncles and drowsy kids until all that's left of this place is a smooth flat lake of mud that hardens in the sun, freezing them all in a moment of terror that lasts until the end of time.

But that's not what happens. What happens is Shane walks home through the rain. What happens is the raindrops unleash the anger he's been pushing away for his whole life. The anger of trying to be a good son, a good nephew, trying to be a good student, a good boyfriend. And once he gets to the city he'll have to be a good Indian. A smart Indian. Not the kind to get lost in a blackout rage or a blackout drunk, but a noble Indian with a sense of humor and sturdy roots twisting back through history.

Shane shoves the door open with his shoulder. He ignores the pots of water overflowing with brown water from the ceiling, and stomps through the kitchen. His shoes leave brown smears on the linoleum. His sleeves drip snaking puddles behind him.

"Mom?"

No answer. He knows where she is anyway. Shane throws open the door to Destiny's room and stands at the foot of the bed. Jackie is curled up in the covers, one arm thrown over her eyes.

"Mom."

Jackie doesn't move.

"MOM." Shane waits. Jackie rolls over, but she doesn't open her eyes. Shane turns around and scans the contents of the room. It's crammed with books, clothes, and old assignments from school. It's a whirlwind nest of his sister's carelessness. Tipped-over bottles of nail polish, a black rose patch she planned to sew on her bag, long-forgotten stuffed animals, all of it teetering on shelves and crammed in corners. When Destiny was here the whole mess of it changed every day like the water. But there's nothing of her in here now. The room seems dead for having been so alive. Shane wonders what Jackie would do if it were all to disappear the way Destiny did. Shane throws aside the curtain and slides the window wide. Light cuts through the room. A blast of storm-damp wind stirs up the dead air. Jackie's eyes crack open. "Close the window."

Shane picks up a stack of magazines and yanks the lamp cord out of the wall before tossing it all through the window.

Jackie sits up with wide eyes, more alive than Shane has seen her in weeks. "What are you doing!?"

Shane rolls up an armful of clothes and chucks them into the yard. Jackie gets up as a family of dolls tumbles out into the night.

"Stop it!"

Shane glares at Jackie. "Is this what it's gonna take?"

He lifts a small shelf, then a bedside table and blankets, heaving everything out into the yard. Jackie picks up a photo of Destiny and her friends from the desk. Shane tries to grab it, but Jackie holds on.

"No—that's from her birthday! I have to keep it for her!"

Shane yanks at the photo harder, and it slips from Jackie's fingers. Shane twists it behind his back. Jackie lunges for it, but Shane blocks her. When he feels the sting of his mother's hand smack across his face, Shane drops the photo. The glass breaks, sending shards of glass skittering over the linoleum.

Shane and Jackie lock eyes. He has her now. This is what he's been waiting for; now she'll have to see him. She'll know how much he hurts. She'll have to be his mother again. She takes his hand and for a moment she's right there with him. Jackie takes a breath as though she's preparing to say something, but then the light in her eyes dims. Something in her retreats. She's gone. Her grip on his hand loosens, and she eases herself down to the ground to pick up the pieces of the picture frame.

Shane watches his mother crawling on the floor with glass in her hands.

"Mom." Jackie doesn't look up.

Jackie examines the photo for marks.

"Mom. Look at me."

Jackie tucks the photo into her breast pocket. "You don't need me."

Outside, Destiny's things spill into the yard like heaps of earth ripped up in the trail of an explosion.

CHAPTER TWENTY-THREE

Shane is huddled under a clammy sheet. The air is heavy, wet, and still. The funeral was a week ago. He's hardly been out of bed since. He keeps his eyes shut, trying to think of good reasons to open them.

Shane's phone rings on the bedside table. David again.

Come outside, David will say. *At least get some fresh air.* And when Shane refuses to come out, David will tell him to call on the ancestors for help. *Lolololololololololol. Right.* When he imagines David's ancestors, he sees a long line of noble elders standing behind him in their regalia, the oldest and toughest Nish army in the history of the world, ready to slaughter David's enemies and smudge their remains. But when he tries to picture his own ancestors, the only ones he can see clearly are Destiny and Tara. Behind them is a threadbare group with stringy hair and shadowy faces. David would say that's because he doesn't know his history, but Shane can't shake the feeling that if it's true that people choose their families (and agree to everything that's going to happen to them over the course of their lives) when they're still in the spirit world, he really fucked up.

*

It takes some time, but Shane eventually pulls himself out of bed. He does a quick email check before his growling stomach drags him to the kitchen. Water from the ceiling drips into overflowing bowls. Garbage and laundry push up against the edges of the room like debris along the shoreline after a storm. Each dish has a crust that won't come clean without a long soak. Shane stands at the counter eating a bowl of cereal. His foot presses against the side of his leg so his knee juts out like a heron.

He got another email from the school this morning. The subject line said *Last Chance to Register!* and there was a picture of happy young people with books walking across the green of the campus. The phrase *Last Chance* blinked on and off in his mind like a marquee. *Last Chance!* It didn't feel like he ever had a chance, so he wasn't sure how this could be the last one. *Last Chance! Last Chance! Last Chance!*

Jackie shuffles past Shane and sits at the table. Shane makes no sign that he notices her. His jaws move with slow directness, as though chewing the soggy-sweet mess into a paste is the most important thing in the world. She lifts the box of cereal and shakes it. A few crumbs rattle inside.

"There's no cereal," Jackie says.

Shane lifts the spoon to his mouth and takes another bite. "So cook something then."

There's a text from Kyle waiting for him when he gets back to his room. *Auntie needs her cut from yr sales. Don't make me come looking.*

Shane tosses his phone on the desk, where the email from the school is still open. *Last Chance!* it shouts.

*

A sheet of gray sky billows over the community center. The breeze is hot like a hair dryer on his face. He's been inside too long. He feels like the top layer of his skin has been peeled away, leaving his whole body raw. Shane flips up his hood and shoves his hands in his pockets.

A few guys around Shane's age have draped themselves on the steps outside of the center. Lyndahl glances over at Shane, but when he sees who it is he turns back to his conversation with Robbie. Shane raises his arm in a wave. If anyone sees, they don't let on. Shane lets his bag slip from his shoulder, feeling the weight dangle from his hand, imagining the package from Debbie sitting inside it like a stone fallen to the bottom of the lake. It would be so easy to walk away.

Shane sets his gaze on Robbie as he steps forward. "Hey, Robbie, what's up?"

"Not much." Robbie glances at his friends. They avoid Shane's eyes.

"You boys need anything?"

"Not from you."

"What does that mean?"

Lyndahl chimes in. "You know what that means."

Shane frowns. He really has no idea but it's starting to freak him out. Did David say something? Do they all know now? It doesn't seem right. "I'm carrying for Debbie so … it's the same as getting it there."

Robbie shakes his head and looks down at the ground.

Shane tries Lyndahl and the others. "Anyone else?"

Lyndahl spits on the ground. The others shake their heads without looking up. Shane slips the strap of the bag back over his shoulder. His phone buzzes with a text. Shane looks down. It's from Ashley:

DIE RAPIST ASSHOLE.

*

Shane sits in Roberta's cramped office with his head in his hands. Roberta watches him closely from behind her desk.

"I can feel you looking at me."

Roberta keeps her eyes on him, waiting for more. "I'm looking at you because I want you to know that I'm here for you. And because you came to my office, so …"

Shane lets his hands fall into his lap. "Don't try to get in my head. Just tell me how I can get money for school."

"I don't think I would want to be inside your head these days."

Shane looks up, trying to assess whether she's making fun of him or just saying something true. Her face doesn't give anything away.

"The school wants the deposit, and I don't have it. I thought I could figure it out, but I can't."

Roberta seems thrown. "I thought you came to talk about Tara."

He knows what she's waiting for, but he's not going to fall apart in front of Roberta. "I don't need to talk about her. I feel like shit. It's fine. There's nothing I can do. I just need to get out of here, Berta."

"I don't know how you can say that."

"Are you going to help me or not?"

"I'm trying to help you."

"No. You're just trying to keep me here like everybody else."

Roberta shakes her head. "Given what's happened with Tara, I'm probably one of the only people who still want you to succeed, Shane."

Shane stands up. "This is pointless."

"People are saying Tara was sexually assaulted before she died."

The back of Shane's neck tingles like a Drift is coming. He does everything he can to hold it at bay.

"You don't seem surprised."

"Should I be?" Shane's hand drops from the handle of the door. "How do they know she was—"

"The police took some samples. There was damage." Images of coroners with scalpels from TV shows swarm in Shane's brain. Cotton swabs, blood, ziplock bags. Roberta presses her palms together, watching him closely.

"Do you think it was me?" Obviously she does. *Why isn't she kicking my ass?*

Roberta takes a breath, choosing her words carefully. "I … know how much you want to go to school, Shane. But if you want my support, I need you to tell me you didn't do it. Once I hear that, I'll do everything I can. Maybe it was consensual?"

All the air comes out of him. Roberta thinks he raped Tara and she doesn't care. She's willing to vouch for him just because he's smart. He knows DNA will keep him out of jail, but she thinks he's a rapist and she's not batting an eye. He feels sick.

"And if I did do it, would you want me to lie?"

Roberta blinks at him and gives him this look like, *Why are you giving me a hard time?* "I'm just saying that I have your back."

Shane's tongue runs over his dry lips. "So ... you'll believe me. No matter what."

"We didn't put this work into getting you accepted at school for nothing. This is just a delay. Next year isn't the end of the world."

Shane grips the edge of the door, thinking of all the times they talked and laughed and made plans for him in her office. She's always been the cool one. Barely an adult, easy to talk to. Full of optimism. The corner of Roberta's eye twitches. She just sold out a dead girl and all that's visible is a twitch. The fluorescent lights buzz overhead. He's never noticed how old they make her look. After a moment, Roberta's eyes float down from Shane and settle on the mess of papers in front of her, like a helium balloon sinking from the ceiling after a party.

*

Shane walks down a laneway behind the center, hoping not to run into anyone. He wonders how long it took for Roberta to look up and notice he had left. Maybe she hasn't even realized it yet. Maybe she'll be there forever, looking at her papers as seasons pass and dust gathers on the surfaces of her furniture, like silt. One by one the hairs on her head will grow gray. Kids will come in and out of her office, spilling their guts to her, and she won't say a word. She'll keep all their secrets, and she'll never call the cops or their parents or their elders. They'll say she's the best counselor they ever had.

"Look who it is." Kyle and Ashley are standing at the top of some steps on the side of a portable that was set up as a *temporary* school library about fifteen years ago. Shane's senses fire out like a net, gathering information in an instant to assess the situation and predict what's next. Roberta would call it an "adaptation to trauma." His tenth-grade science teacher called it the "fight or flight" instinct. It seemed like a no-brainer to Shane. Given the choice, he'd pick flight every time. If he could sprout wings from the knobby bones in his shoulders right this second, he wouldn't hesitate.

Ashley stomps down the wooden steps. "You make me sick. Why would you even show your face around here!?"

Shane steps back. *Rapist.*

Ashley takes a swing at him, but Kyle holds her back. Her closed fist passes with a rush of air over Shane's cheek. "Fuckin' creep!" Ashley yells. "She was my best friend!"

She was my friend too! Shane wants to shout back, but it's not the time. Kyle's arms are locked around Ashley, but the smirk on his face is daring Shane to give him a reason to let Ashley loose.

Shane takes off down the lane, imagining the crunch of gravel growing faint as his weight is lifted off the ground and his wings beat the air above him.

*

Shane spots the car sitting in front of his house from a block away. It stands out, black-and-white like a life-size porcelain zebra on their lawn. Jackie once bragged that the cops had never been to their house. But then Destiny died, and they had to come by a bunch of times. And then they brought Shane home after he found Tara.

Shane stops. *Why are the cops at my house?* As soon as the question occurs to him, panic starts kicking in his chest. There's only one reason. If the cops only visit his house after a suicide, then ...

Mom.

Shane's whole body screams out for him to run home. To break down the door and demand to know what happened. But he forces his legs to take slow, measured steps. If the cops are there, then it's already too late. He pulls his shoulders back. He would rather get there holding his head up. The cops have seen enough of his tears.

But when Shane gets closer, Jackie is standing on the porch talking with two officers. *Alive.* Jackie looks past the officers and locks eyes with Shane as if saying, *You're not safe here, my sweet boy.* The officers have their backs to him. He can still get away. Shane spins around and runs. Every slap of his feet against the dirt sounds like:

WHAT-TO-DO

WHAT-TO-DO

WHAT-TO-DO

The answer is rattling around in his bag. *Debbie.* He hasn't sold anything yet, but that doesn't matter. He can propose to be her guy in the city. No one knows him there. He'll dodge the cops here, go down to the city, get set up, and he'll have her paid back in no time. *YES—that's it.* He turns onto the road that leads to Debbie's and picks up speed.

Debbie slides a fifty-dollar bill into the gap between her bottom teeth, clearing out a stringy bit of jerky from earlier in the day. When she's done, she wipes her fingers on her sweats and smooths the fifty onto a stack of red bills.

Debbie looks up. "What, no coffee this time?"

"Nope. Too broke." Shane tosses the packet of drugs on the counter in front of Debbie. The gesture feels less dramatic than it was when he imagined it on the way over. Debbie doesn't even glance at it.

"What do you want me to do with that?"

Photos of Destiny and Tara cast looks of judgment at him from Debbie's shrine. Shane is suddenly uncertain. Shane mumbles at the ground, "I can't sell it."

Debbie scowls. "That sounds like your problem, not mine. I need to get paid."

"But nobody's buying from me, Deb!"

"You can sell it and pay me, or you can keep it and bury it in the ground for all I care, but I still gotta get paid."

Shane is drowning. Everything seemed so clear when he left the house, but now his mind is scrambled: a TV flashing between stations. He hears Jackie screaming when she found Destiny's body, Roberta's voice promising to believe him no matter what, Tara's eyes pleading for him to stay, Uncle Pete telling him in a million ways that he will never be the right kind of man. But then there's David, his face tilting up to kiss Shane, the sound of his breath like the hushing of rice stalks; David whispering *I love you* into his ear. It's enough to make Shane feel the weight of his feet against the ground again.

He looks up at Debbie. "I have a better idea. And if it works,

I'll make way more for you than I ever could here." Shane checks Debbie's reaction. She's listening. "I … if you loan me the money to get to the city, I could start selling for you at university. It's gonna be full of rich kids and …"

Debbie barks out a "HA!" Just the one syllable to let him know she's laughing before the scowl settles back on her face. "YOU're gonna sell for me down in the city? You think the people who run shit down there are gonna let you open up shop?"

"Maybe."

"What, you think because you got good grades and you got a little boyfriend that makes you special?" Debbie snorts and barks again, "HA!"

How does she know about me and David!? The TV in Shane's brain goes nuts again: Tara hanging from the rafters; his sister lying dead, her face blue and something crusted around her mouth; Destiny's floating feet when she danced jingle; Tara's voice calling out, *Please don't leave!*; his first beer with Uncle Pete in the summer sun; the cops at his front door; Ashley heartbroken, *She was my best friend!*

Kyle appears from behind the shed, and the mess in Shane's head falls away. Everything makes sense. That's how she knows. *Kyle.* It had to have been him. The only way Debbie could have found out is if Tara told Kyle that night. Kyle, the one who never made a secret of wanting her, the one who can't handle hearing the word no …

"Word gets around, faggot," Kyle sneers.

"What did Tara say to you?" Worry flickers over Kyle's face. That's all Shane needs to see. Shane takes a step forward. "It was you! You were with her that night. You did that to her."

Debbie heaves herself up from behind the counter like a mama bear protecting her cubs. "Prove it."

Debbie picks up a bat and walks toward Shane. "I was with my nephew all that night. And anybody that says different is a liar." Shane backs away. "Now get me my money, before I send someone to beat it outta Jackie and that little butt buddy of yours."

Shane dodges behind Debbie and reaches out to grab the photos of Tara and Destiny down from Debbie's wall of death. The pictures tear a bit at the corners, leaving scraps pinned to the board, but it doesn't matter. As long as Debbie doesn't have them.

CHAPTER TWENTY-FOUR

Moths launch themselves out of the darkness like a nightmare blizzard, desperate to get to the buzzing light above David's door. Shane has been here for hours, hiding in the bushes outside, waiting for night to fall and trying to figure out what his chances are that David might let him in. He hasn't heard a word from David since the day of Tara's funeral. Shane wouldn't blame him if he slammed the door in his face.

The moths flock to the light, beating their wings against the white-hot bulb again and again until they can't anymore. *Doesn't matter how much of a survivor you are,* David thinks, *something shitty is always coming for you. And you'll survive it just like you survived the last one and the one before that until the really bad thing—the thing that can't be beaten down or fought back—finds you. And that's it. At least those moths die together while reaching for something bright.*

Shane takes a step out across David's yard and settles into the beat-up couch outside the back door. If he's too scared to knock or text to let David know he's here, at least Shane can come out in the open and let himself be seen. That way David can decide for himself whether or not he wants to come outside and meet him halfway.

After what must be an hour or more, the door squeaks open. David walks out with a bag of garbage held in front of him. Drips from the garbage darken the boards of the deck when he passes Shane. No words, no eye contact, no acknowledgment at all. *That's it. That's my answer.* Shane collapses into the lumpy, mildewed couch, straining for air. He's tried to go home, he's gone to Roberta, and even to Debbie. There is nowhere else to go. He is alone. Really alone for the first time in his life. Shane sobs into the fabric of the couch and grinds his face into it like a kid having a fit. After a moment, he feels his body begin to lift away in pieces like a boat splintering against a rocky cliff. It might be the beginning of a Drift but this feels darker, new. When an arm slips around his shoulders and draws his pieces together again, he expects to see Destiny. Dark eyeliner smudged at the corners, that lopsided smirk that could mean *I love you* or *I'm just messing wit you.* But it's not her. It's David's eyes —no trace of a smile—hovering beside him.

"How long have you been out here?" David asks.

The flood of relief drowns out the question. Shane curls into his lap. His body shakes with tears.

"How could they think I did that to her?"

David strokes his hair. "I know. Shhh … it's messed up. But they can't pin it on you. "

A wave of tears takes him again. "I'm so sorry. I don't know what I'm doing."

David kisses the top of his head and whispers into his ear. "It's okay. You don't have to do anything. I got you now."

The two sit in silence for a long time. David closes his eyes and runs his fingernails over Shane's scalp. After a while, Shane stops trembling and his breathing becomes regular. It feels right to be held by David. The night air strokes their skin, cooling all except the places where their bodies press against each other, alive there with damp summer heat.

*

Evie is camped out in front of the flickering blue fire of the TV. The door creaks open behind her. "David?" Evie calls.

David comes in and snuggles beside her while Shane stays glued to the shadows beside the open door, waiting for a moment when Evie's distracted enough not to notice him sneak in.

"Did you talk with Janice about selling our rice at the store?" Evie asks.

"Ah, no … not yet. I'll do it tomorrow."

The cordless rings from Evie's lap, making her jump. "Oh!" She laughs. "I forgot I put that there." Evie raises the phone to her ear.

"Hello?" She frowns. "Anybody there?"

David watches her face. "Why don't you just hang up?"

Evie tilts her head and fumbles with the holes in the afghan the way she used to do with the telephone cord before David replaced it with the new one a year ago.

"Jackie? Is that you?" Shane's mom was the only one Evie would ever talk to on the phone past six, but it's been weeks since they spoke. After a few moments, Evie hangs up and sets the phone in her lap.

"Was it her?" David asks.

"She hung up without even saying anything." Evie grabs the remote and turns the volume up on the TV. Behind them, Shane creeps down the hall and into David's room.

*

A few minutes later, David slips inside and closes the door behind him. "Do you think we should talk about … ?" Shane pulls him into a kiss. No, he doesn't want to talk. Right now all he wants is to be as close to David as possible.

Without a noise, the two strip off their clothes. Their need draws the air from the room. It creates a vacuum where sound is impossible. No air to tremble. They kiss and bite and tease each other in perfect silence until all that's left is the telltale dribble running down David's stomach. They lie in the heavy summer heat, lungs expanding and hearts beating in unison. A train rumbles in the distance, letting sound rush back into the room like light into the dark.

Shane curls into the curve of David's back and whispers in his ear. "We're going to be like this every night soon."

"How?"

"I don't know. But we will."

*

The morning light eventually reaches across the edge of the lake and comes crawling over David's sheets. Shane sits on the edge of the bed in his underwear staring straight ahead at nothing.

He's spent the night chewing on his problem like a piece of gristle. *I need to get away, but to do that I need money. There's no way to make enough money. But I need to get away, and to do that I need money. But there's no way to make enough money.* The other problem, the one he hadn't thought of, is that he has never broken the rules. Not really. Even trying to sell for Debbie wasn't that big of a deal really. A guy gets ambitious, he needs something, so he builds himself up on the backs of his people. It's not the Anishinaabe way, but it's what lots of them do now. In some ways it's what people expect. *I'm just tryin' to get mine,* he's heard people say. What Shane hadn't thought of until right this second is, what if there is a way to help himself by bringing down the people doing the most damage in the community? What if he is willing to do something illegal and dangerous but ultimately … good? People will say he just did it for the money. They'll call him a thug, a disappointment, but what if what they say doesn't matter? What if good is good? *Could he do it?*

Shane gets up from bed, watching himself in the full-length mirror like a cat stalking a bird. He locks eyes with himself and brushes a bit of fluff from his cheek. He squints like he's staring into the sun.

"Gimme all your money! Now!" Shane whispers. *Not scary enough.* Shane backs away from the mirror and adopts a tough-guy stance, with his fingers pointed at the mirror like guns. He tries again. "Gimme your money!" He breaks into a giggle. "Gangsta-aaaaaaa." Shane tries to relax his body, but he can't. There's too much adrenaline pumping through him now.

David rolls over, rustling the sheet. "What are you doing? Come back to bed."

Shane jumps away from the mirror. He almost forgot about David. "I was just playing around."

David looks at him strangely. "You seem better."

"It's 'cause I'm a genius." Shane wonders how much he should give away, but if they're going to be together in the long run they'll have to trust each other.

David laughs a little and rubs his eyes. "Okay …"

"What if we could get our money for Toronto and stop people drinking and doing drugs?"

David makes a noncommittal sound.

"No, but listen," Shane continues. "If we could find a way to do that, we should do it, right?"

"Yeah. Okay," says David. "But it's impossible."

Shane smiles. "If you can't get a solution, create an explosion."

*

When David hears Evie close the bathroom door, he seizes the opportunity to duck out into the kitchen for the stone mortar and pestle that Evie uses to grind up medicines. Back in the room, he hands it to Shane. Shane's eyes follow the ropy vein that runs down David's bicep and curls over the muscles of his forearm.

"What?" David asks.

Shane grins. "Aren't I allowed to look?"

David blushes and sets the mortar and pestle down in front of Shane. "This is such a bad idea."

"No, it's a great idea." Shane smiles and kisses David with a familiarity that is sweeter than anything either of them could have said to each other. Shane steps away and shakes a fistful of pills into the bottom of the mortar.

"You better not kill my *nookomis* with that shit," David says.

"It'll be all cleaned out before she knows anything happened." Shane taps at the pills with the pestle, breaking them into large pieces while David gets ready to leave. Shane leans into the job, putting the force of his weight into crushing the hard tablets. How far did they have to travel to get to Evie's mortar and pestle? Opiates that were mixed up in a lab who knows where, then shipped to a drugstore and sold to someone in pain who turned around and sold them to a dealer, passing from hand to hand until they ended up with Debbie and now Shane. How much money has been made by getting these pills (and others like them) up here to burn a hole in the community his family has called home since the beginning of time? And now he's here, calling on their power for money just like the rest. Shane pushes the powder around with the pestle, hoping the good medicine that Evie mixed up in the mortar will somehow lend its goodness to his plan.

A soft shuffling comes from the hallway. Shane didn't hear the bathroom door open again, but it must have. David puts a finger to his lips, then turns to watch the strip of light under the door. Sure enough, two shadows appear and then pause. Shane pictures David's *nookomis* leaning in to put her ear against the door to listen. By her own admission, Evie didn't live this long and become so well respected by minding her own business.

"David? You still home?"

David hesitates. "Uh ... yeah."

Evie rattles the knob. "It's locked."

"I'll be out in a minute."

Shane watches the shadowy blobs from Evie's feet, but they don't move.

"If you want to know something, you can ask me, you know," David says.

A small grunt sounds from the other side of the door and the lumpy shadows retreat. The sound of a faint radio, CBC North, can be heard coming from the kitchen.

David picks up his backpack. "Are you sure you're going to be okay by yourself?" Shane doesn't really want to be left alone, but there are things that he needs to prepare for tonight, and he isn't about to go cruising the rez right now. Not as long as the cops are still trolling around looking for him.

"Nah. I'm good."

David nods and puts his hand on the doorknob.

"Hey." David stops. "Where's my kiss?" David leans down and presses his lips against Shane's forehead.

"I love you," he says. Before Shane can reply, he's opened the door. David covers Shane's mouth with his hand to keep him quiet, gives him a last look, and shuts the door behind him.

Shane can hear him and Evie in the kitchen.

"Slept late today?" Evie asks. It sounds like David doesn't answer. Shane imagines him picking up one of his sneakers, concentrating on acting casual. He probably looks more like an alien anthropologist that's wearing his body as a skin suit in order to pass himself off as a "local Indian boy" before reporting back to the mother ship about sconedogs, status cards, and tipi-creeping.

"When did Shane get here?" Evie asks.

Shane cringes.

"Ah, it's just me," David mumbles.

"Oh, I thought I heard him in there with you."

Shit. Shit. Shit. Stay strong, David.

"It's probably just the TV."

He can hear David fumbling with something—*his shoes? Doesn't matter.* The weather stripping makes a sound like a burst of static when David opens the kitchen door. Shane smiles to himself. If Evie does know something, she must have decided not to badger David about it, which is almost as good as her not knowing at all.

"See you tonight."

Shane moves to the window so he can watch David trudge down the walkway and away from the house. Shane imagines Evie watching him from the living room on the opposite side of the house. They are mirrored halves of the same body, each with their own hopes pinned to David.

*

Shane turns back to the pills, now a fine white powder in the mortar. He carefully scoops it out with the handle of a spoon and transfers it back into the little baggie. It doesn't look like much now that the pills are all ground up. He sees that some of the powder is still stuck to the small scrapes and scratches inside the mortar. Shane smacks the side of it with the palm of its hand to dislodge the last bits of powder, but what shakes loose isn't even worth trying to get into the bag.

The doorknob rattles loosely. Shane freezes. Two shadowy lumps have appeared in the band of light below the door. How long has she been there? Did he make any noise? The doorknob rattles again. Shane holds his breath until Evie shuffles away.

Once she's gone, Shane takes stock of the room. There isn't anything left to do until the sun goes down. He fishes around in his pockets for the pictures of Tara and Destiny that he rescued from Debbie's shrine. The creases add lines to their faces that make them look older than they'll ever be. *How could he not have seen?* But of course he saw. It's just that they didn't seem like they were hurting any worse than him. It must have been different, though. Their pain has to have been darker and harder than the prickly bundle Shane carries with him. Because if it's the same, what then?

Shane tries to smooth the picture of Destiny on his thigh, but the folds are pressed too deep. Destiny killing herself will never make sense. That's what other people do. Other kids' sisters, not his. But does it seem impossible because she didn't leave any clues, or because he wasn't paying attention? He saw her every day. He shared a bathroom with her, cooked meals with her, went to the same school. He *was* there. No one liked to say it, but some of it had to be her own fault. If she never said anything, how was he or anyone supposed to help her? Can he really be responsible for the lives of everyone he loves? It's too much. Icy panic rises from Shane's stomach, inching toward his throat.

Fuck her. Fuck her for leaving me alone like this. Fuck her for thinking her feelings were so private and so hard that she couldn't even reach out to her family. Fuck her for not loving any of us enough to stay.

Shane crawls into bed, surrounding himself with David's smell, feeling sick with the desire to run but unable to escape. All of this is supposed to be about school—at least it started that way—but he finds himself caring less and less about the idea of going to class, learning about zoning bylaws, sewage treatment, and the whole network of policies that create a functioning community. Every time he thinks of getting away, he imagines holding David's hand while they stroll by the water, like something out of a cheesy commercial. But what if they walk away from here and the only thing either of them has left is each other? Will it be worth it? His mom and Evie may never speak to them again. He's heard of two-spirited people being welcomed back into their communities, but he can't picture it. Those people must have had different families, different lives, a set of magical circumstances that made it possible. Shane pulls aside the curtain. The robin's-egg sky is slashed with bright white brushstrokes of cloud. A group of kids zip by on bikes, screaming and laughing at one another. There is magic here, just not the right kind.

He hasn't been away from Jackie for this long since Destiny died. He would bet money that she's been calling the police every few hours to make them promise they'll call her as soon as they take him in for questioning. Once, when Shane was about eight, he and Jackie took a trip to Kenora for a couple of days. They stayed with his auntie Cher, not a real auntie but a friend of his mom's from when she was a girl. They lived in a big housing complex full of Indians from all over the north. Kids ran back and forth between the apartments, hardly noticing whose house was whose, eating and playing until one place ran out of good snacks or they got bored of the toys, and then heading on to the next one. Just like at home, but with way more people squeezed close together. There was an older boy who hung around there named Thomas.

He wore sleeveless T-shirts to show off his handful of scraggly armpit hairs and he openly smoked in front of the adults. Nobody bugged him about anything. He was terrifying.

On the morning they were supposed to leave, Thomas called Shane over. He knew his mom would want to hit the road in the next little while, but he couldn't say no. Thomas chatted him up for a few minutes and then told him to follow him to his house. He set up his game console and announced that they were going to play strip *Mortal Kombat*. Every time one of them lost a match, they would have to take off a piece of clothing. Shane had never played the game before, but there was no way to refuse. Shane threw everything he had into the game, using the old press-all-of-the-buttons-as-fast-as-you-can-and-hope-it-does-something trick. He lost a lot, but for every game he lost, Thomas lost one too. It was weird, but Shane wasn't going to question it. Before long, both boys were naked and Thomas was proudly doing tricks like making his penis spin around in circles by doing a little hop and wiggling his hips. He had never been allowed to look at another boy's body so close before. And here Thomas was, not only letting him look, but encouraging him to. The doorbell rang but Thomas said they could just ignore it. It was while Thomas was showing Shane how he could walk across the room with a whole dollar in nickels stuffed inside his foreskin (he said he could get all the way up to two dollars) that Jackie walked in. She had been hunting for him for hours, ringing doorbells and making everyone crazy. In a panic, Jackie had run around peeping in the windows of apartments where no one answered when she rang the bell. And that's when she saw them.

Jackie didn't speak while he gathered his clothes and said

goodbye to Thomas. They got into the car and watched the rows of town houses slouching by. As soon as they hit the highway, his mom began to cry so hard that she had to pull the car over. Shane apologized over and over, but the tears kept coming. Between sobs Jackie said, "It felt just like when we lost your dad." Jackie shook in his arms. Shane could only think of one thing to do. He started singing "Don't Worry, Be Happy" in the weird muppet voice that they made up when he was learning to talk. When she started to sing, he knew it was going to be okay. But the whole ride home, Shane couldn't shake the feeling that something had changed. He had depended on her for everything, but he never thought about how his mom might need him too. Being loved that much was terrifying. What if one day he couldn't give her what she needed? Would she fall apart again?

Maybe that was why Destiny was able to make herself do what he had never been able to do, no matter how desperate he felt. She thought her life was hers alone to live or to end because she never had a moment when she saw just how badly they needed her. When she was alone with that emptiness, when she lost sight of the shore, Destiny might have imagined her death like a burned-out bulb on a Christmas tree, a small spot of darkness no one would notice in the chaos of sparkling lights on every side. There was no other way she could have done it. Not if she knew what it would do to them.

Shane rubs his arm. A constellation of pink scars dots his shoulders where his mother's fingernails dug into him on the day Destiny died. He runs his fingers over the smooth half-moons. Now that Jackie has fallen apart, she's not his responsibility anymore. He can't save her because she's already gone. Having nothing to lose isn't the same as being free, but it might be the closest he'll ever get. Shane sits up in bed. The pads of his feet spread over the floorboards, primed like a sprinter waiting for the starter pistol. Once David gets home and the sun dips past the tree line, they will be unstoppable.

CHAPTER TWENTY-FIVE

When they step outside, the sun hasn't been gone long. A shred of violet softens the edge of sky that curves around the scrappy western tree line. Stars scatter through the sky like glitter from a cannon. Shane and David walk along the road without speaking. The windows of the houses glow like campfires. Shane can't remember another time when his brain and his spirit and his pure animal body pulsed together like this. It's like watching someone else control his body from a distance. He feels like himself and someone else at the same time. Is he transforming, becoming stronger, or coming apart?

They get all the way to Janice's store before David realizes that he left the rope behind. Shane doesn't want to go back. They might lose momentum.

"Don't puss out on me, David."

"It's still early, we've got all night." David is already turning back. "I don't wanna fuck this up." Shane looks longingly at the lights of the store winking at him, flirting through the trees. The night feels charmed. Nothing can go wrong. David walks back the way they came.

"Fine," Shane says. "But no excuses next time."

When they get home, the lights in the kitchen are on. Evie should be asleep by now. She never turns the light back on after nine unless she's got a guest over. They creep up to the edge of the windows, but the curtains are shut tight.

"What now?" David asks.

"I'll go in and out through the bedroom window. There's no way she'll hear."

David looks back at the house, full of panic.

"What else am I supposed to do? We can't go in, and we can't go to Debbie's without the rope."

Shane boosts himself up to the edge of the window, trying to remember what he might knock over on the dresser when he slides in. Thankfully there's not much there other than a torn ribbon shirt David's been waiting to mend. Shane slides the window open and shimmies inside. The ribbon shirt drops to the ground with an airy *plop*, but otherwise the room is quiet.

When Shane stands, he hears voices coming from the kitchen. He stays still, listening. It sounds like his mom, but that would be impossible. Jackie hasn't left the house in forever. Shane steps closer to the bedroom door and presses his ear against it. The cheap plywood door vibrates like the skin of a drum.

"You're sure they're together?" Jackie asks. Her voice is watery but clear enough to make out.

"I heard them talking in David's room this morning," Evie says. Shane blushes, wondering what else she might have heard. The women go quiet. Shane imagines the two of them together at the table, searching for the right words in their mugs of hot tea.

"How long do you think it's been going on with them?" Jackie again. Shane holds his breath. *She doesn't know. They can't know.*

"It's not right," Evie says. "Ask me, the creator made men and women different for a reason. To make babies, you know?"

Shane has heard versions of this line for his whole life. Lessons about the traditional roles of men and women. Lessons about the importance of keeping the worlds gendered and distinct as a way of honoring the teachings, as a way of honoring ourselves and our ancestors. The pairing of male and female as the only way to achieve balance. Rigid rules with no room for him or David. Rules that cut them out like something sick.

"When he was a baby, an elder from James Bay told me Shane would be two-spirited," Jackie says. Shane's heart leaps. He's never heard anyone he knows say the words *two-spirited* before, much less his mom. He's read it online but ...

"I tried to raise him up normally. I hoped that elder was wrong and for a while he seemed okay, but now I don't know."

"That's for city people. *Gichi-mookomaanag.* We don't do that here," Evie says. The ice-water panic rises to Shane's throat again, numbing his whole body.

"When he and Tara got together, I thought that was behind us."

"You think maybe he made David that way?"

It's as though a string connecting him to the women's voices suddenly snaps. Like something vital has been severed. Shane looks down at his hands and feet to make sure he's all there.

Jackie and Evie continue to murmur on the other side of the door, but he can't listen anymore. He's imagined versions of telling his mother so many times, preparing himself for the sadness he expected to feel once she knew. He's surprised to find that sadness is only a small part of it. The anger is much bigger. *Who is she to cut me out after promising she would always be there?* Shane picks up the coil of rope from the floor and slips out the way he came.

*

When Shane drops down into the grass beside the house, David is nowhere to be seen. Shane circles around to the back, but the yard is empty. He would call out if he wasn't afraid Jackie and Evie would hear. Shane circles the house and finds David, crouching beside the kitchen window, listening to the women's voices inside. His face is tight and gray. Shane whistles softly to catch David's attention and swings his head toward the road. When David doesn't move, Shane curls his hands into two half-moons and presses them into the shape of a heart against his chest. David takes a last look at the light peeking through the curtains before he joins Shane in the road. Neither of them speaks about what they heard. Shane reaches out for David's hand, then thinks better of it and tucks his own hand back into his pocket.

They slip between houses and through little shortcuts in the bush to avoid being seen. Since the cops are still looking for Shane, he hides behind the propane tanks while David heads inside Janice's store. Shane looks up at the sea of stars, willing himself to float above his body, feelers groping for signs of danger. It's the first time Shane has been able to Drift while still maintaining control of his body, both inside and outside of it at the same time. It's like watching a character on a TV show and wondering what they're going to do, even though you've already seen the episode a hundred times before. But this isn't TV, none of this has actually happened yet. He has the power to stop it at any time. But he won't. Their plan is on its feet and racing through the rez on padded paws. It's all he can do to keep up.

David comes around the corner with a coffee in his hand. "I got it," he says.

"Triple-triple?" Shane asks. It's the only way Debbie will take it.

David nods. Shane takes his elbow and pulls him deeper into the shadows. They creep behind the building and around the back way, avoiding the loose knots of younger kids who wander in packs through the yellow pools of streetlight. They might as well be on a whole other planet tonight.

Before he died, Shane's dad used to watch an old movie about a couple of white guys in suits called *The Blues Brothers*. They were trying to get a group of musicians together in order to make money to save a convent, but Princess Leia and the Nazis kept trying to blow them up. Shane's dad always said the most important lesson in life was in that movie: *No matter what happens, just be cool.* The Blues Brothers said they were on a mission from god, so they knew that anything they did would work out in the end. That's how Shane feels now. His shadow self is guiding them from above, which may not be as good as a mission from god, but it will have to do.

"What if Debbie's not there?" David says.

Shane scans the darkness without responding. There's no point. He knows she'll be there.

"She could be closed too. Sometimes she goes partying in Brickport. Ashley told me she's got a guy over there ..."

"Shhhhhh! It'll be fine."

Shane wonders if it was a mistake not to talk about what Jackie and Evie said. David seems different since they left, but Shane can't risk opening up a conversation that might derail everything before they even began. And it doesn't matter now. David can have all the doubts he wants, just as long as he plays his part.

*

Shane feels the bass throbbing from Debbie's speakers as they pick their way along the unlit back road that leads through the junkyard behind her compound. The humped roofs and hoods of abandoned cars are piled on either side like the rocky walls of a ravine. Shadowy graffiti creeps along the doors like the marks of their ancestors, ancient pictures that say, *This is me. I am here.*

An old RV is parked on the edge of the compound, hiding David and Shane from anyone within the circle of light that spills from the porch. Debbie is sitting in her usual spot, exactly where she's supposed to be, tucked away behind the counter in front of the shack. The portable TV gives her face an immortal, bluish cast.

Kyle and Ashley are on the couch at the edge of the light. It's closest to the trailer he and Debbie sleep and eat in. It used to be in front of the porch where Debbie sells from, but Kyle moved it against the main trailer so that girls would have fewer steps to change their mind after getting up from the couch and walking to Kyle's bedroom. He didn't like being that close to Debbie and her legendary mouth anyway. The crazy thing was, moving the couch closer to his bedroom actually worked. At least, if his bullshit was to be believed, he got laid a good 25 percent more often than when the couch was in the old spot.

David rests his hand on the side of the RV. "I feel like I'm gonna puke."

"You're not. Just take deep breaths. Everyone is where we thought they would be. We just have to wait until Kyle and Ashley go inside to fool around."

"What if they don't go in?"

"Don't puss out now, David. You want to make things better, this is your chance."

David leans against the RV and closes his eyes. "You don't need to say shit like that to me. I know why you're doing this. Don't pretend like it's some kind of noble mission."

Shane scrambles to come up with the right words to make David stick to the plan.

"Don't worry, I'm not quitting." David rubs at his eyes. "What should I ask her for?"

Shane lets himself breathe again. "It doesn't matter," Shane says. "Get whatever you want."

Kyle pulls Ashley up from the couch and guides her toward his trailer. After a few moments, fresh beats shake the walls of Kyle's bedroom.

"It's time," Shane says, and takes the baggie of white powder out of his pocket. He squishes the bag between his fingers. There are still a few chunks that he wasn't able to bust up with the mortar and pestle, but hopefully it's not enough to tip Debbie off. By the time she gets to the bottom, those Oxys will have her right fucked-up and she won't notice.

Shane opens the seal and shakes the powder into the coffee. The white mound floats for a moment before it disappears into the cup. Shane works up a gob of saliva and lets it dangle above the surface of the coffee for a moment before he lets it drop into the drink.

"You're sure this is safe?" David asks, as Shane stirs the foamy wad with his finger.

"She's selling it. If it's not safe it's her own fault." This is either the smartest or the stupidest thing he's ever done, but he's having too much fun to know the difference. "You're up," Shane says, and passes David the coffee. David hesitates for a moment, then takes the cup.

"You can do this, David. And no matter what happens, she deserves it. Right?"

"If I shit myself, it's your fault." David takes the coffee and steps into the clearing at the center of the compound.

Debbie turns down the music and calls out to him before he gets halfway to her table. "Come this time of night, you better have a coffee in your hand!"

David raises it up. Debbie gestures him forward. Shane creeps closer, still hidden by a patch of low bushes. He can just barely make out what they're saying.

"So what do you want? You've never been here alone before. You even drink?" Debbie asks.

David pauses. And then his pause stretches out, becoming something else. He forgot what he was going to ask for. *Just say something,* Shane thinks. David turns to the price list on the wall.

"Um ..." David says. *Okay, good start,* Shane thinks. Debbie has a frown on her face like David is the biggest idiot she's ever served, and Shane knows that's not true. She must know something's up. "Do you have any champagne?" David asks.

"You got a date with that faggot friend of yours tonight?" David freezes. Debbie looks back, stone-faced. "You know what, I don't wanna know." Debbie hoists herself up from the chair, frowning as though, instead of champagne, David had asked her for gay porn. Shane smiles to himself.

Debbie turns from David and rummages around for a bottle.

David glances back at Shane's hiding spot, looking twitchy.

Debbie heaves herself from the back corner with a bottle of sparkling wine in her fist. She plops the bottle on the counter and grazes the cup of coffee just enough to send it spinning off the edge.

"Aw, Christ!" Debbie says. "Can you grab me another one?" Debbie leans over to mop up the spill.

"I …" David watches her like a kid who's dropped an ice cream on the sidewalk.

"Never mind. You got the thirty?"

David holds out a handful of bills. Without looking up, Debbie takes them and stuffs them in her bra. Her rag moves in slow, deliberate circles over the counter.

"You can go."

She doesn't have to tell him twice. David scurries into the dark like a mouse that's escaped a cat's claws. When he gets to the RV, David ducks behind, holding the bottle close to his chest.

"She spilled it," David says.

"I know. I saw."

"And the safe is closed."

Shane pokes his head out to watch Debbie. She takes a last swipe at the counter and tosses the rag into a corner. She's breathing like she just got back from a run. Shane tries to think of the last time he saw Debbie anywhere other than right there behind her counter, but he can't. By the amount of effort it took just to clean up that spill, it doesn't seem like she could get very far at all.

Shane smiles at David. "It's okay, we're still good."

"We're definitely not good. We can't do anything with her awake."

"It's two against one. What's the worst that can happen?"

"Are you kidding? She knows us!"

"So? She's gonna turn us in for robbing her illegal business?" Shane looks at David, wondering how far he can push him. "This is it, David. We're gonna be gone soon. Just us, nobody else."

"I'm not doing it."

"What?"

"It's too crazy, Shane. I can't."

"I'm doing this for us, David. I love you."

"Well, don't do it for me. I'm already home."

"Didn't you hear your *nookomis*? They don't want us. Not the way we are."

David juts out his chin, suddenly defiant. "Fine."

Shane takes a step back, a car spinning its tires on an ice road, nowhere to go. *One less person to lose.* Shane kicks the side of the RV with his full weight, making the old siding clatter.

"What's going on over there!?" Debbie calls, squinting into the dark.

Shane pushes away from the RV and plows through the clearing. When he glances behind him, David is following a few feet behind. "Go home, David!"

Debbie rises from her seat. "I thought I told you to stay away from here!"

In a few short steps, Shane is behind the counter. He reaches around Debbie's neck with one arm and grabs at her wrists with the other. The clammy plucked-chicken skin of Debbie's neck slides beneath his palms. "Jesus Christ! Get off!" Debbie chokes.

David steps forward and backward in an idiotic dance, unsure of what to do or where to go. He reaches for the cash box from the counter and holds it to his chest. Debbie shoves Shane against the wall, trying to shake him off.

"Open the safe!" Shane shoves the back of Debbie's head down, forcing her to her knees.

"I can't open nothing with you holding me!" Shane reluctantly lets go of her arms. Debbie fiddles with the combination lock.

"Let's just go!" David pleads.

Shane knows he's right. It isn't too late. They could run across the grass and down onto the highway; they could speed together over endless stretches of cracked pavement, past an infinity of hardscrabble trees and fields of runny-egg-yolk flowers. The trouble is, when he imagines them stopping, they both disappear. The only way for them to stay alive, even in his imagination, is to keep running.

The safe clicks. Shane turns back to Debbie, catching a glimpse of a gun and a bag of cash that she's pulled from the open safe. Debbie stands and tries to turn around. David sees the gun and dives out of the way. Shane ducks around Debbie, grabbing both of her arms from behind.

"Get the hell off me!" Debbie swings wildly, trying to knock Shane loose.

The trailer door bangs open. "Auntie, what the fuck is going on!?" Kyle is standing there in a beat-up pair of boxers, one hand over his crotch.

Debbie kicks at the wall, sending her and Shane tumbling backward down the staircase. Sometime mid-fall, her gun goes off. The shattering *crack* of it doesn't sound like thunder or rocks breaking; it sounds like what it is. Debbie and Shane hit the ground, and Kyle slams to the gravel moments later, screaming and clutching his shin.

The bag of cash is close, but just out of reach. Shane scrambles to his feet and lunges for it. Just as Shane gets a grip, Debbie hauls herself up and manages to get a corner of the bag in her hand. Shane springs forward with it, but Debbie is stronger than she looks.

"Gimme back my money!" Debbie grunts.

They wrestle with the bag, and the plastic splits, scattering bills into the field. Shane swipes a few bills and grabs the gun from the ground before Debbie starts barreling toward him. Better in his hands than hers.

"David, run!" Shane quick-steps backward and pivots around, darting over the grass. David is already a handful of steps ahead, legs pumping toward a wall of darkness, his body flailing into the void. At this point, Shane's memories more than his eyes are guiding him to the bottom of the road. Far behind them, Kyle is still screaming.

For a little while longer, it's just the way Shane imagined. Just him and David. Feet and pavement like the very first drums. Breathing hard—rattles keeping time. Grandmother moon winking in the star-freckled sky. Trees like ancestors with their arms held high. Shane lets out a long howl. The dogs answer back, sending them both into a fit of manic laughter. David stumbles and stops to catch his breath.

Shane jumps up and down, full of adrenaline, the gun bouncing at his side. "I can't believe we just did that!"

David coughs and spits.

"C'mon! Let's go!" Shane slaps David on the shoulder.

"Where are we going!?"

"I don't know!" Shane tugs on David's shirt and drags him down the street, both of them laughing, stumbling over each other as they jog.

In the distance, the cry of sirens gets louder. Shane smiles. He wishes he could see the look on Debbie's face when the cops show up to find her out front with money scattered everywhere, a safe full of drugs, and Kyle bleeding in front of the trailer. She can try to hide some of it, but she'll never be able to hide it all before the police arrive.

CHAPTER TWENTY-SIX

The air by the lake has a surprising bite. Mist rolls up off the sun-warmed water like steam off a bowl of moose meat. Shane stops running at the shoreline. There's nowhere else to go. When he left Debbie's place his footsteps felt like they were launching him into flight, but he's in freefall now, bracing for the inevitable moment when the ground rushes up to crush him. David's steps echo behind him.

They stop at the water, panting like dogs. The run has turned Shane's stomach inside out and left his chest burning. His dry tongue sticks to the roof of his mouth and his heart shakes everything in his body at once. Something dark in him is waking up, like a shapeless toad dragging itself out of the stiff mud in spring.

David coughs. "How much did you get?"

Shane waves a single twenty-dollar bill in the air and lets out a jittery laugh that dies on the air. Shane's body clenches, sick. Twenty dollars. That's a cheese pizza. That's a two-pack of underwear at the mall in Dryden. *Fuck.* Is that what all of it was for? Tara, Destiny, Jackie, David—all gone one way or another. Is that how it ends? He should have ignored Roberta. He should have ignored his stupid dreams and kept himself small. Because if you shoot for the stars and don't make it, no one will forgive you. *You can do anything.* What bullshit.

"Oh god." Shane looks up at David. "I fucked up. I'm poison. I'm fucking poisonous to everyone." Shane fights back a sob that comes from his guts. David reaches out for his shoulder, but it's tentative.

"Don't touch me!" Shane jerks away, searching David's face for some sign of betrayal. After all, this is what David must have wanted all along. He never wanted Shane to leave, and now he's trapped. No school, no Toronto, no girlfriend, no need to come out. He's got them frozen in rez-time forever.

"I know you're happy," Shane says. "You win—nothing fucking changes!" Shane shoves David, sending him tumbling back onto the ground.

David's eyes are wide "I'm not happy! How could I be happy!?"

Shane doubles over. The soil heaves and swells beneath his feet, like water. His guts are coils of muscle pushing for his throat. The pressure of Debbie's gun against his thigh is the only thing clear and real. Everything else spins out into the blur of space. The protective skin that keeps him from crossing into the spirit world has never been thinner. Like a balloon under a faucet, it grows and stretches tight with the weight of both worlds pressing from both sides, threatening to split open. He wishes it would. It would be easier there. It has to be. Shane pounds the side of his head with his fist. There's a flash of pain and then a rush of relief moves through him. *Relief.* Shane pulls his fist back and cracks his head again, clearing the darkness with blasts of pain until all that's left is dizzy white fire. *No thoughts. No feelings. Free.*

"Shane!" David takes a step forward, and then stops. He's afraid. Shane slams his fist against his own head again and again. *Everything is a lie. They're all liars. They told him he was smart. They told him he was special, that he was going to do great things. He let them down. He's not good enough. He'll never be good enough* ... Shane keeps punching. David screams at him to stop, but he can't. The pain is shaking something loose. His hand tightens around the gun.

David reaches out to him but Shane lurches away from David and charges into the lake, sending up a spray of water like fireworks all around him. The lake wraps itself around his thighs. His waterlogged pants cling to his body like a drowning child. David charges after him.

"Go away!" Shane calls.

David keeps on coming. Shane pushes into deeper water, the gun raised above his head. He stops and puts the gun to his temple. He feels a lurch and suddenly everything disappears but the black water and the pressure of David's hands holding him under. His arms push back at David, flailing for life, but the truest part of him is already somewhere far away. Drifting.

There is no sound here. Nothing but emptiness, and then a flash of Destiny's face, her laugh. And then his mother is holding him with hands that smell like tomato vines. And David. His pulse, his teeth, his heartbeat. And then all of it disappears. The skin ruptures. The barrier to the spirit world opens wide and ... no one is there. No Destiny, no Tara, no smiling father to meet him. But he's not alone either.

His body feels strange, like he's being brushed with feathers. He is dissolving. Cell by cell. Not vanishing, but melting like the creek's crust of ice in spring. Not carried away by the current, but carried deeper into the world, filling the spaces between the molecules of the earth, the air, and the water, with life. His own life. It's like seeing the whole world and being inside the skin of every creature at once. Like hearing all the songs and dancing all the dances, living the lives of every person, every rock, every tree at the same time. But as more of him is drawn into that stream, as he begins to feel himself joining the pulse of his ancestors—the secret beat underneath them all—Shane pulls back. One day he will have to walk this path; that much is guaranteed to everyone who lives and breathes. But if he takes this path now, his pain won't die with him. It will pass to the ones he loves the most. Just as Destiny's pain did when she went to the spirit world, Shane's pain will become his mother's pain. But it won't end with her; it will fall over the community like ashes from a volcano, blanketing everything, becoming part of everyone from the oldest among them to the ones just born.

He wishes he could walk through the world so lightly that he'll never make a mark, never hurt anyone, or take up space. But it's impossible. He changed the world the moment he took his first breath and his mother kissed the top of his head. Being alive changes things. It just does. He can choose to do good or bad, but he can't do nothing. Everything he says and does matters. Living is a choice. Dying is a choice too, but dying is a choice that affects more than just himself. It's a choice to hurt the ones he loves. Seems like the only way out is to live, no matter how much it hurts. And the only way to live is to discover what he's capable of, to find a way to be of use. Because this is the only story of himself that anyone will ever know—his only life—and there's too much left untold. The ancestors will be waiting when his time comes.

With a rush of air in Shane's lungs, the world comes back. The lake. The moon. The rice. The stars. Shane is cold and shaking, coughing up water. David is already trudging back to shore. Shane watches the gentle lurch of David's back, the angle of his lowered head rounding his shoulders forward, his neck parallel with the ground. Shane has never loved him more. David finds a spot close to shore and lowers himself to the sand. He wraps his arms tightly around his legs and presses his forehead to his knees. The lights of the powwow grounds glow behind him.

Shane walks to the shoreline, feeling the darkness drain out of him and into the water of the lake. The gun is somewhere deep, covered with sand, already beginning to rust. Shane collapses on the shore beside David and rests his head on his shoulder. David doesn't move. His body feels like stone.

"I'm sorry," Shane says. He knows it's not enough but it's all he can offer.

David keeps his eyes out on the lake, but reaches out for Shane's hand. Shane takes it.

"Never again," Shane says.

David squeezes Shane's hand and curls into his lap. The moon is gone now. The night has nearly exhausted herself. A haze of lavender is beginning to glow behind the trees at the east end of the lake. Another day is coming.

CHAPTER TWENTY-SEVEN

Shane doesn't remember taking off his clothes or crawling under the covers with David, but when he opens his eyes again, David is asleep with his face pushed against Shane's shoulder. The house is quiet except for their breathing. Shane turns to check the time. The digital clock blinks from 3:59 to 4:00 p.m. Once when she was making pie, Jackie told him that 4:00 was the perfect time of day. It's late enough that most of the work is done and there is still time yet for an evening of laughter. She called it the balancing time, poised at the center of the medicine wheel, a moment suspended in perfect balance. Four directions. Four seasons. Four o'clock. When she told him about the balancing time, it made Shane sad to think that his mother only ever got one moment to feel good each day. As though reading his mind, Jackie had told Shane there would be periods when the balancing time could be flattened and rolled out like dough: that our lives, like our days, revolve in cycles, and that there would be days—even whole years of his life—when he would feel like he was living under the blanket of the balancing time. Like every moment was as perfect as four o'clock. Shane laughed and told her she was too young and good-looking to be talking like an elder.

My balancing time started after you were about one.

Not when I was born?

Jackie laughed. *No, that first year was nuts. I never slept.* Shane smiled and watched her pour the bowl of bouncing blueberries into the pie shell. Their juice splattered red flecks along the raw edges of the crust. Jackie smoothed the berries over with her fingers and tucked them in like sleeping babies under the pale skin of dough. She stepped back to examine her work, then said, *The balancing time ended the day your dad's boat went down.*

He hadn't asked. He didn't want to know. *You might have another time like that. Maybe it's starting right now.*

Jackie had pulled the oven door open and set the pie inside. *It might. But I'm not holding my breath.*

That was years ago. Destiny was alive and everything felt possible. Maybe that day was the beginning of another balancing time. He never asked about it again, although he did tease her about it whenever he noticed that it was four o'clock. *Balancing time, Mom! Better get your giggles in!*

A pot clangs in the kitchen. David shifts under the covers next to Shane, pulled up toward the surface of his dreams by the sound. After a moment, he lets out a sigh and sinks back down. Shane steps out of bed and puts his ear to the door. He can hear something sizzling in a pan. The house had been empty when he and David arrived home, but his mom and Evie must have come back while they slept.

"How long are we gonna let them stay in there?" he hears Evie ask.

"They need to rest," Jackie says.

"Are they in the same bed?"

Jackie shushes Evie. Shane imagines his mom puttering around the kitchen like she used to.

"They're too young. They don't know what they're doing," Evie mutters.

"They're home. That's all that matters."

Shane waits with his ear pressed to the hollow door for another minute, but they're too busy cooking to say anything else.

He turns away from the door and takes in his bedroom, as if seeing it for the first time. The beige walls are plastered with images of fancy cars and maps of Toronto, London, and New York. The space has never felt smaller than it does right now, with maps of the world's great cities closing in on him as the smells of coffee and bacon curl toward him like a memory of better times. It makes him want to puke. All that time spent dreaming and hoping and wanting something that there was no chance he would ever have. And what was it that he even wanted? Money? A life like the ones he's seen on TV? To feel smart and accepted by people like Roberta, who urged him on with the weight of their own lost hopes? He was shooting for something that no one could define in concrete terms, except to say, *NOT THIS. This life isn't good enough. Life on the reserve isn't good enough. The place where I'm from isn't good enough. My family isn't good enough. My teachings aren't good enough. I'm not good enough. But if I go to school and learn something "useful" maybe one day I might be good enough, and then I can show the other Indians how to be good enough too.*

Shane yanks at a corner of the map of Brasilia, then rips the paper in two. The bird-shaped city drops to the carpet. It feels good. He snatches the other large maps from the wall. They *crack* like thunder, knocking smaller transit maps and pictures down with them. The last to fall is the homemade collage of watches, houses, and luxury cars that Roberta had him put together for his "wealth wall" back when she was getting kids to visualize the physical things that they wanted from life.

David opens his eyes and turns toward the noise of falling paper like he's under attack. "What time is it?" David asks.

"Like, four o'clock."

David rolls over and rubs his eyes. "Looks like you're giving up."

"Doesn't matter now, does it?" Shane flops down on the bed beside David. "I'm too fucked-up to leave, even if I wanted to."

"You don't want to go?"

David's question settles in the space between them. David probably wants him to say he doesn't want to leave, but the truth is he doesn't know what he wants. He wants to rest. He wants to breathe. He wants to take his time. The sound of Jackie and Evie laughing buzzes through the door.

"Is that my *nookomis*?"

Shane nods.

"I better go."

David throws on a shirt and lifts up the window sash to leave.

"She knows you're in here."

David glances out the window, eager to go. "Just tell her she's hearing things. Nothing has to change."

"Nothing has to change?"

"I still love you," he says. But when he says it, the words sound more like, *Can I go now?* Or, *Please don't be mad at me.*

Shane holds David's eyes, making sure that he's listening. "I love you too. But if you go out that way like you're ashamed or something, you can't come back." David glances at the door to the hall then back at Shane, like he's trying to figure out whether Shane means it.

Shane leans forward and picks a rumpled T-shirt from the floor. He wants to hug David and tell him everything he wants to hear, but if he starts lying now it'll be the end of them. Shane shakes out the shirt and slowly pulls it over his head. He pricks his ears and angles his body toward David, trying to make it easier for David to say, *No—stop, of course I'll come out with you.* David stays frozen with his eyes fixed on the door, listening to the sounds from the kitchen: a spoon on the rim of a bowl, the clatter of plates. Evie's low laughter.

When Shane is fully dressed, he turns to David and reaches out his hand. All he has to do is take it. David teeters like he's considering a dive from a cliff. In or out. Now or never. Shane steps forward with his hand outstretched. After what feels like the longest moment of his life, David reaches out and takes it.

*

When they step out of the bedroom, the kitchen looks better than it has in a long time. It still needs work, but the piles of garbage and the stacks of crusty dishes are gone. Evie is mixing up a bowl of bannock with blueberries. Jackie leans against the counter with a cup of coffee. It feels too good to be true.

"What are you doing?" Shane asks.

"What's it look like?" Jackie says. "You boys go sit down." Evie frowns and shakes her head a little. She's noticed Shane's and David's fingers twined together. Bad eyes or not—she doesn't miss much. Jackie shoots Evie a warning look, but neither woman says anything.

Shane takes David to the table, unsure whether to be relieved that neither his mother nor Evie seems to be in the mood for invasive questions, or pissed off that they are ignoring what feels like an important moment. It took guts to come out here together. Couldn't they at least acknowledge it? *If his mom and Evie thought they could pretend that nothing happened …*

"You were gone when we came home. Where did you go?" Shane asks.

"I was at Evie's. Where were you?"

"Out."

If she's not going to say more, neither is he. Evie's whisk sings against the inside of the bowl, soaring over the wet *plop* of beaten eggs.

"How do you want your eggs?" Jackie asks.

Shane stares out the window. David jumps in. "Scrambled, please."

Jackie waits for Shane's response. Shane looks at her blankly, not letting it go. "You pay the store yet? Janice isn't gonna wait past today."

Jackie shakes her head. "I'm not paying her."

Shane's head snaps up. "What does that mean?" He watches her like a dog that's been offered a bit of meat, hungry but wary.

"I'm gonna move," she says. "This house is way past repair, even with the money I planned to spend."

"Okay but …"

"Evie and I worked it out so that I could live with her and David while you're at school."

"So my inheritance money is still there?"

Jackie tosses a debit card on the table. "You can see for yourself next time we go into town."

Shane picks up the card and runs a finger over the raised letters of his name. "Even with the inheritance, it's not enough."

Jackie shrugs. "It buys us time. I'm sure we can figure it out for the second semester. Once they know you, maybe we can apply for scholarships and …"

Shane shakes his head. "You can't do this, Mom. We've lived here forever."

"But this way you can go to school."

"What, you're just gonna let it rot and fall in? Nobody gives up their house, Mom. You can't."

Jackie sits down at the table. "Janice can sell that stuff to someone else. And Evie's got room." Jackie smiles at him expectantly.

Shane frowns. She thinks she's solved all his problems. Like she can run away from him at the exact moment that he falls off a cliff, then come back later and stitch him up like nothing happened.

"I thought you would be happy."

Shane lifts his head to meet his mother's eyes, but the closest he can get is her mouth. Any closer and he'll lose it. He's needed her for so long that, now that she's here, looking at him the way she used to do, everything wants to come out in a tumble, and he's frozen. David is rigid beside him, waiting to hear what he will say. Shane tries to slow his brain down and focus on his options. He can tell his mom that yes, he is happy, then thank her and make plans to move to Toronto to go to school. But that would be a lie.

He could tell Jackie that he's been hiding pieces of himself for longer than he can remember, and that he's been performing the role of Heroic Young Straight Son, Future University Graduate, Future Nish Leader for so long he doesn't know who he is or what he wants anymore. But that's not all there is. Because if he's really being honest, he would have to help her understand that he hasn't stopped moving since Destiny died. He's been circling around and around, losing himself in pain because in some way it's right. He *should* be sad. He should be guilty. They all should. They let Destiny down. He let Tara down too. He hurt her to save himself and there is no making that right. He will have to carry that grief until it's as much a part of him as the land he was born on.

But all that is too much for Shane to say. That darkness is packed hard inside him like a wad of wet leaves in a drainpipe. If he pushes to get it all out at once, the words will spew out in a tangle of pain that'll only do more damage. He'll have to take his time, letting it out piece by piece.

"I ... can't go. Not right now." Shane speaks without looking up. "Maybe next year or something but ..."

"You don't have to decide right away." Jackie puts her hand on his. "It's your money either way." Shane can't remember the last time her hand covered his like that. Shane's body relaxes. The warmth passes in a wave from David's hand on one side and his mother's on the other, filling him up like a transfusion of blood.

Evie shuffles away from the stove with a pan of eggs. She clears her throat loudly, and David yanks his hand away from Shane's.

"I just heard scrambled, so everybody gets scrambled," Evie

says as sits down next to David. Jackie takes the handle of the pan and dishes some eggs onto their plates. Shane takes one and passes it down to Evie. When all their plates are full, silence settles over the table. Steam rises off the pale eggs. Butter melts into slabs of blueberry bannock. Soft light seeps greenly through the leaves of the birches outside. No one moves to eat, as if they've all lost their appetites at once.

Shane gets up and crosses the kitchen. The others watch him open the cupboard and lift down another plate. Shane returns to the table and offers it to his mother. "Can I do a spirit plate?"

Jackie takes it from him gently and scoops a bit of eggs, a piece of bannock, and a slice of orange onto the plate.

"Shane, put a sausage on there," Evie says. "Your sister loved those."

"Should I take it outside?" Shane asks.

"You can take it to the water after. I'd like it here with us for a bit." Jackie sets the plate in the middle of the table.

Evie picks up her fork and smiles. "Let's eat."

CHAPTER TWENTY-EIGHT

Drugs Lead to Rape Arrest

After reports of gunshots, police arrived at the residence of Debbie Maanendan (35) and Kyle Maanendan (23) of Ishkode Ojibwe Nation. When officers arrived on the scene, they found Mr. Maanendan bleeding from a gunshot wound. A search resulted in the discovery of a hidden stash of illegal narcotics with a street value of over $20,000. An undisclosed sum of cash was also found at the scene. Both Debbie and her nephew Kyle Maanendan are in police custody and are expected to be charged later today.

Kyle Maanendan has, however, already been charged with sexual assault causing bodily harm against a 17-year-old local girl, who later committed suicide. Police say they were tipped off by the girlfriend of the accused, Ashley Chandler, after she found an article of the victim's clothing in Maanendan's bedroom. Police would not confirm whether Maanendan is a match for the attacker's DNA sample, but they have taken him into custody and charges were laid early this morning.

CHAPTER TWENTY-NINE

There are deep furrows in the carpet that outline the place where Shane's desk and bed and bookshelf used to be. Shane crouches down to lift the last box and carries it out of the room. There will be space for most of their things at David and Evie's house, and the rest can get donated. It didn't take long for people to calm down once the cops took Kyle and Debbie away. A few of Kyle's cousins made noise about coming after Shane and David, but when most of the community came to their defense, the cousins backed off.

Shane breezes through the bare hallway and out the front door. He's walking taller and his back is broader, as if coming out to his family has given his body permission to grow. Jackie picks up a bin of odds and ends from the kitchen and follows Shane down the driveway. She looks stronger, steady. Her eyes never stop moving, as though taking in all the little things still left undone and making lists in her head.

Pete gives Shane a long look up and down, squinting at him from the back of his truck. "Only one box? Man, what kinda load is that!?"

Hot red splotches spread up Shane's neck and into his cheeks. Pete knows how to get to him every time.

"Aw, leave him alone." Jackie laughs.

Shane wipes at a bit of sweat running down his temple. David takes the box from Shane and gives him a peck on the cheek.

"Still sleeping alone, Uncle?" David grins and passes the box to Pete. Pete squirms, but he keeps his mouth shut. It's incredible—a month ago Shane would never have imagined they could joke like that in front of his uncle.

Evie teeters down the steps behind them, her arms loaded with boxes. "Ever lazy, Pete!" Evie calls out. "Just organizing things while the women and boys haul boxes." Shane and David leap forward to take boxes from her. Evie brushes her hands off on her skirt and gives the boys a wink; she's just giving Pete a hard time.

"Jesus. That better be the end of it." Pete slams the tailgate closed.

Jackie pulls a twenty-dollar bill out of her pocket. "Why don't you head down to the store to grab some lunch? We're gonna clean some things up here."

Pete takes the money. "It's a waste of time, Jacks. Nobody's moving in."

"You just go eat. Let me do it my way," Jackie says.

"You're the boss, I guess." Uncle Pete slides into the cab of his truck and pulls away. Jackie turns around and walks back to the house alone.

"Mom?" Jackie doesn't stop. Shane, David, and Evie pass uncertain glances between themselves.

Shane takes a deep breath as he crosses the threshold into the kitchen. Everything is gone—all the dishes and baking pans, even the smells that made the place belong to them have disappeared. What's left is the anonymous scent of kicked-up dust and mold that every abandoned house has. Like when a noisy pile of Aunties and half-asleep kids leave a party, and suddenly the low hum of the fridge and the creaking joints of the building grow louder, filling the space that the people have left behind.

Shane's footsteps echo off the walls, unnaturally loud. The living room looks smaller with nothing in it. His mom is standing at Destiny's door. Shane slips his arm around her waist and looks into her room. It's untouched. The rest of the house is like a skeleton picked clean by animals, but her room is like a zombie— alive with the memory of Destiny's life and death. A still-open wound, made worse by the fact that half of it is still strewn across the backyard. No one picked it up after Shane threw it out. It's been heating up in the sun during the days and gathering dew at night. Shane rests his head on his mother's shoulder.

"Do you want us to box up Destiny's stuff until we do a give-away?" he asks.

"We're not doing a giveaway," Jackie says.

Shane nods, but it doesn't make sense. Every time he thinks his mom is back to her old self, she says or does something that doesn't seem like her. A giveaway is a chance for people to grieve and to remember, to take a piece of Destiny with them, something to remember her by. A giveaway is what people want; it's what they expect. And it's what Jackie needs. She hasn't spent time in ceremony in too long. Shane can't help feeling like she would come back to herself if she could only find a way to pray again.

*

The chipboard at the back of Destiny's bookshelf slaps loosely against Shane's knuckles. It's hard to get a good handhold. He and David maneuver it down the hallway and out into the yard, stopping several times to adjust their grip. They would both have splinters by now if it weren't made of only sawdust and glue.

"Do you think we're doing the right thing?" David asks.

Shane isn't sure. "Why? Are we going against some serious Nish teachings or something?"

"I don't think so but ..."

"Yeah. I know."

They set the bookshelf on the ground and David pushes it over, letting it settle on top of a pile of things from Destiny's room. They had started with her mattress against the grass, then heaped on clothes, jewelry, posters, drawings, birthday cards, and books. They added little things Destiny made, gifts she was given and forgot about, school assignments and toys from when she was small. They piled it piece by piece until her room was empty and all the physical evidence of her life was stacked so high it spilled out over the sides of the mattress. Seeing his sister's things dragged outside feels wrong, as though Destiny might come running out of the house any second, pissed at him for messing with her stuff.

David rests his head on Shane's shoulder. Shane keeps an eye on the house. He can see Evie through the open window of Destiny's room. Evie shuffles past the naked walls, saying a prayer in Anishinaabemowin and fanning the smoldering medicines with an eagle feather. The smoke wafts up, drifting through shafts of honeyed light. When Evie finishes her prayer Jackie steps inside the door. Evie offers her the sacred medicine, but Jackie shakes her head. Evie knows better than to offer again. She touches Jackie's shoulder and leaves her alone. Jackie stays there for a moment before she moves to the center of the room. She crosses her arms tight and keeps her eyes fixed on the floor. It hurts to watch. After a moment, Jackie raises her head. Her hands reach out for the bald walls, caressing the thumbtack holes with her fingertips. When she steps back to the middle of the room, Jackie slowly turns, taking in the emptiness of Destiny's bedroom, gently circling the space like a dancer searching for her partner.

"Hey." David squeezes Shane's hand. The contact brings him back to himself. David brings Shane's head to rest on his chest. Shane closes his eyes and leans into it. Until now they've been careening from one crisis to the next. It's hard to imagine what being together will look like without fireworks and pain. The quiet feels uneasy.

Evie picks her way carefully over the grass. She focuses on her shuffling feet, careful not to trip. David releases Shane's hand, leaving him alone and adrift.

Evie squints up at them and pushes her glasses higher on her nose. "Boys."

Uh-oh. Here it comes. She hasn't said anything about them being together yet, but she doesn't have to. It's in the way she puckers her lips when they sit too close, and the way she clears her throat when she sees them looking at each other for too long. And they both heard her the night they broke in to Debbie's. *We don't do that here,* she said. *Creator made men and women different for a reason,* she said.

Evie fixes her eyes first on Shane, and then on David.

"*Nookomis.*" David looks like he might cry. It takes everything he has to both honor her and stand strong with Shane.

"Shhhhh…" Evie reaches up to David's neck and pulls him down to face her. She kisses his forehead gently, then lets him go and steps over to Shane. He bends down so she can press her lips against his brow, gentle and dry as the brush of a bird's wing. Evie takes both of their hands in hers. She closes her eyes and a tremor flutters over her face, the kind of trembling that begins deep underground before the earth moves. She squeezes her eyes tight and presses Shane's palm into David's. Evie holds them there together, letting their bodies disappear into each other at the place where their skin touches. When she opens her eyes, she looks at them for a long moment. *I see you. Your ancestors see you, and they're happy.* Tears burn Shane's eyes. Evie lifts their clasped hands high into the air and holds them there. All at once the trembling stops, and a smile opens Evie's face.

Shane doesn't know how long his mom has been watching, but suddenly Jackie is there with them. She puts her arm around Shane's waist and steps out of her shoes. Shane and the rest of them follow her lead. It feels right. And all at once they're in ceremony, connected to one another, with their feet in the soft earth. Something is beginning.

Jackie steps forward and nestles a photo of Destiny on top of the pile. It's a rare photo of her with a real smile. Jackie must have snapped it mid-laugh, just before Destiny's hand came up to cover the crooked tooth she always tried to hide. Staring down at the picture, Shane thinks that nothing has ever felt so enormous and looked so tiny at the same time. Shane takes a photo of Tara out of his pocket and places it beside Destiny. In the picture, Tara's hair has been swept to the side, and her chin juts out like she's been given a dare she isn't ready for. Shane takes a deep breath. He doesn't know if he can do this. It's too much to ask. He takes a step back and joins his family for a moment. There is always a chance that Jackie will change her mind about the plan. Jackie strokes his head, then passes him a box of matches. Shane looks up at her. Jackie nods. It's time.

Shane crouches down low. He pulls a match out of the box and rolls its rough square edges between his fingers. He scrapes the match against the sandpaper. The match flares with a *crack* that cuts through the sound of the wind and the waves. Shane watches the orange light travel toward his fingertips, blackening and twisting the wood as it moves. He touches the match to the corner of one of Destiny's drawings and the fire passes out of his hands—no longer his. The flame creeps its way over clothes and furniture, slowly nuzzling her things as if asking permission before consuming them. And she must give it, because within moments the flames seem to be everywhere at once. The outside of the cardboard boxes darken and peel back. The flames rise.

Jackie presses her head against him. Both their faces are wet with tears. When his mom told them she wanted to burn Destiny's things, he didn't think it was right. It seemed angry, destructive, *not our way*. But all prayers can have their place, if they come from a feeling that's real and comes with good intentions. And if nothing else, Destiny's life deserves an event to mark its end. Not a ceremony that the elders would do; not a droning sermon at the church; not a celebration of life at the bingo hall. Something that Destiny herself would be proud of. Something fierce and reckless and free.

They stand watching the fire grow, holding their ground even when wave after wave of heat tightens their skin and stings their faces. The pain is part of bearing witness.

Jackie takes a deep breath before she speaks. "Shane—you can do anything, you know."

Her voice vibrates in his chest and spreads through his whole body. Shane nods. *She's right.* For the first time since he can remember, he isn't terrified of what the future holds. He doesn't have a plan and he doesn't need one. For once, all paths are open and there is no pressure to choose.

He tilts his head to the sky, imagining the cool touch of Destiny's fingers on his cheek as the ashes are lifted, curling into the clouds. Something inside him has come loose, like a red leaf in fall.

Goodbye, sister. For a moment it feels like he might pull off on a Drift. It would be so easy to disconnect from his body and follow those ashes as far away as they will take him. But he doesn't need it anymore. Shane lets out a breath and leans into the warmth of his mother and David and Evie. A pulse drums through all of their bodies as they stand by the fire, rooted together, strong. Shane pushes back on his heels and digs his toes into the warm dirt. He is exactly where he needs to be.

ACKNOWLEDGMENTS

This book would not have been possible had it not been for the army of people involved in developing and producing the film, *Fire Song*. The film took years to get off the ground, beginning with development support from Sarah Kolasky and Elke Town. The film would never have gone a step further without Laura Milliken, PJ Thornton, and Michelle Derosiers, who were there in the trenches throughout production and are still helping to get *Fire Song* out in the world. Thank you most of all to the communities of Fort William First Nation and Wabigoon Lake Ojibway Nation (particularly Donna Chief and the whole Chief family) who opened their doors and allowed us to tell this story on their territory. And thank you to Donna for reading the book and giving me your thoughts. To the cast of the film, thank you so much for letting your spirits shine through and giving these characters life. I heard your voices in my head every day while I wrote the book, so you have continued to inspire me long after the film was complete. Many thanks to Eden Robinson, Lee Maracle, Thomas King, and Richard Wagamese, who gave me the confidence at the Banff Centre for the Arts to try writing prose. Thank you to the Ontario Arts Council's Writers' Reserve Program for supporting this project, and to Sheldon Suganaqueb for helping me come up with the name of the community where the story takes place. Thank you so much to Rick Wilks and Katie Hearn at Annick Press for suggesting that I write this book. I will be forever grateful for your support. Lastly, thank you to my husband Ryan and my stepdaughter Rose for all that you give me every day. I met you in the hazy days after wrapping production on *Fire Song* and I've been in a haze of love ever since.